# This Cowboy Took Me Away

Linda R. Boggess

# Contents

# Chapter 1

My name is Charlotte Dutton - Charlie, for short. I am the youngest child of John and Evelyn Dutton. My father owns the largest ranch in Montana - the Yellowstone Ranch. One day, it will be up to us - Lee, Jamie, Beth, Kayce, and me to run it, and keep the legacy going.

I would say that I have a decent relationship with my siblings. Some relationships are better than others. Kayce is my twin brother, and growing up, he loved to remind me that he was twelve whole minutes older than I was. When we were kids, Kayce was definitely a momma's boy, but it was definitely fair to say that I was a daddy's girl. I always preferred doing ranch work, or working with the horses than almost anything else.

When it was time to choose a career path, my dad really pushed for each of us to do something, or become something that could help the ranch. Lee stayed home, and learned how to run the ranch. Dad pushed Jamie into law school. Beth went into the business sector. Kayce ran off and joined the military after he found out he was going to be a father. I chose to go to veterinary school, so I could come home, and be the vet for the ranch.

I came back a couple years ago, and now Lee and I share a house on the grounds of the ranch. I didn't like the thought of being in my late twenties and still living with my dad. Lee was the least objectionable option at the time, and it oddly worked out.

Things seemed to be going okay for the ranch until Dan Jenkins came to town, trying to build condos and a resort right next to the ranch. Looking back, it seems like everything went to hell all at once...

The day before Lee died was a good one. Kayce brought his son, Tate, up to the ranch to see Dad. Originally, I wasn't going to go with them when they moved some bison to a different pasture, but Kayce asked, and I couldn't say no.

I saddled my horse, and rode her up to the main house, before dismounting, and tying the reins to the fence. I looked over, and saw Beth's car in front of the house. "When did Trouble come home?" I asked.

"You never left," I heard her reply over my shoulder.

I turned around to hug my older sister. "You always did come in like a tornado," I said as we pulled apart. "Who's the unlucky victim that brought you back to town?"

"Not sure yet. Dad called, and here I am," Beth replied.

"Interesting," I nodded. "I don't remember the last time all of us were here together," I mused.

"It's been years. I didn't see you in the house last night; where do you stay?" Beth asked, raising an eyebrow at me. "Is there something I need to know."

I laughed, "There's nothing you need to know. Lee and I share a cabin. It just felt weird living in the main house."

"Doesn't seem to bother Jamie," Beth commented, judgment seeping through every word. Her feud with Jamie was no secret - but whatever the hell started it, sure is. I've asked a hundred times, and neither of them will tell me.

"Charlie!" I turned with a huge grin on my face when I heard Tate call my name.

I dropped to my knees and opened my arms for him to run into. "Tater Tot!" I giggled, hugging my nephew. "You're getting so big! How's your mom?"

"Good."

"You ready to ride today?" I asked, standing back up.

"Duh!" he laughed.

I looked up at Kayce, "It's been too long," I said, hugging my twin brother. "You look good."

"So do you," he replied. "Monica says hi."

"Hi back. You ready to go?" I asked, gesturing back to the horses.

"Let's go!" Jamie called, already on his horse.

"Want to tell me why we're moving bison?" Kayce asked, after he'd helped get Tate up into the saddle with our dad.

"Your guess is as good as mine, at this point," I replied, pulling myself up into the saddle.

"Morning Charlie," Ryan said, as he got up onto his horse. He was one of the cowboys, and a reserve livestock agent.

"Morning Ryan," I smiled, and kicked my horse in the belly and pulled back on my reins to back my horse away from the fence.

I wasn't shocked to find out that Beth was not joining us. I don't think she's been on a horse since our mother died. "I can't believe you're not in court today," I giggled, riding alongside Jamie.

He shook his head, "I couldn't say no either, when I heard he was coming home."

"Some family time won't kill us," I teased.

Jamie raised an eyebrow at me, "I beg to differ." He relented when I glared, "Alright, aside from Beth, the rest of you are tolerable."

"Oh good, for a minute there, I thought you hated us," I replied sarcastically.

"Just her."

"Why?" I asked.

"Because she's horrible."

I shook my head, "Please get a girlfriend, or just go get laid. You've got a lot of tension that you really need to release. I think it would do you a world of good."

"Is that your professional opinion?" Kayce asked with a laugh, coming up on my right.

"Yes!" I replied.

"Wanna race, like we used to?" Kayce asked, once we finally got the bison to their final destination.

"Oh, you're on!" I kicked my horse without warning and ran off before Kayce said he was ready to start.

"You always cheat!" he yelled, easily catching up to me.

"Then you should know better at this point," Lee called.

Once we were done, we left the bison with the cowboys, and went to go fishing in a nearby river for lunch. The boys had already decided, and invited me when I was about to head back to the barn.

"I don't remember the last time we all did this as a group," I mused, casting my line into the river.

"I don't think we ever have," Jamie replied.

"Sure, we have," I replied, but when I stopped to think about it, I couldn't recall a single time. Plus, Beth would never do this with us. It was sad. I glanced over when Lee handed his pole to Tate to reel in.

"You've got something on the line there," Kayce pointed, snapping me out of my thoughts.

I reeled mine in, and volunteered to go to the banks and start a fire so we could cook our catches. I got the fire started, and wrapped my fish in the foil and put it over the fire. I did the same when Tate and my brothers brought me their catch.

"This is a good day," Tate sighed with a smile.

"Yeah, it is," I replied, cutting into my cooked fish. I wasn't squeamish about it.

Whenever we get together, just us siblings, we tend to give each other a lot of grief. Everything was fair game. After Jamie and Lee gave Kayce crap about leaving the ranch, they turned on me - or I should say, Lee did.

"Did I really catch you foolin' around with one of the cowboys in the barn last night?" he teased.

I felt my face turn red, "You saw that?" All we'd done was make out a bit, but nonetheless, it's embarrassing to be caught acting like a teenager.

"More than I cared to," Lee replied.

Kayce choked, "Does Dad know you're sleeping with one of the cowboys?"

"We haven't slept together," I snapped, taking a bite of fish. "Who I'm seeing is none of his business, or yours for that matter."

"Which one was it?" Jamie asked, looking over at Lee.

"Low man - Ryan," Lee smirked.

"Could be worse," Jamie laughed.

"Your face is so red, Charlie," Tate chimed in.

I could feel the heat radiating off my cheeks.

"We're just teasin', Charlie. If he makes you happy, I say go for it." Kayce said.

"Yeah," Lee nodded.

"Just don't get him in trouble. We're both adults," I said.

"We won't say anything," Jamie agreed.

"Thanks."

That was the last good day I had with all of my brothers together. I'd been hearing rumblings about cows wandering onto the Broken Rock Indian Reservation, but I hadn't paid a lot of attention until there was a full tactical team leaving the ranch. The repercussions for

Kayce - who lives on the Reservation with his wife, Monica, and Tate, - didn't occur to me until it was too late...

# Chapter 2

Everybody left the ranch in the early evening. I'd come up to the house at the end of the day because I noticed a large group of people gathered up close. I saw Lee in his bullet proof vest, carrying an assault rifle, and ran to catch up with him. "What's going on?" I asked. "You look like you're prepping for war."

"We kind of are," Lee replied.

"What does that mean?"

"Well, my group is going to get those cows back off of the Reservation," he explained as we kept moving.

"And the other group?"

"Diverting a river," he said dismissively.

"Oh, okay," I replied, like that was no big deal. Colby, one of the ranch hands, strapping a crate of dynamite to a horse, did not escape my notice.

Lee told me not to bother with making dinner, because he'd be really late. That was the last thing he said to me... "Don't worry about dinner. It's going to be a late one."

I felt a deep sense of dread as I watched everyone leave, including my father, who was leaving in the chopper. I gave Ryan a small nod as he rode by, following Lee's group out to the main road.

Rip, my father's most trusted soldier, was leading the second group of people.

"Good luck," I said, as he passed.

"We'll be fine, Charlie," Rip replied with a nod.

I walked up to the porch when everyone was gone, and sat in one of the chairs, looking out over the fields. Beth stepped outside a while later, and sat down in the chair next to me. "Do you have some aversion to coming inside?" She asked.

"Just don't feel like it," I shrugged. "Are we alone out here?" I asked, looking up at her. It was eerily quiet, and it just didn't feel right.

"No, Jamie's inside," she replied, sitting down in the chair next to mine. "But otherwise, I think so."

We sat in silence for a bit, until it got dark. Neither group had come back to the ranch yet. "Do you ever get the feeling that something bad is about to happen? Like, something bad is about to happen, and there's nothing you can do to stop it?" I asked, looking over at my older sister.

"No," Beth said, shaking her head. "But it's freezing out here. We can wait for them inside." She stood up and motioned for me to come with her. "Come on, Charlie. I'd put good money on the fact that you haven't eaten since breakfast, and you're starving right now."

"You don't cook," I mumbled.

"No, but Gator said leftovers are in the fridge," she told me. Gator is the cook who works in the main house. Usually, I cook for Lee and I because by the end of the day, neither of us feel like going up to the main house to eat. We'd only go up for special occasions - or if there was something that Dad really needed all of us at the table to discuss.

"If I go in and eat something, will you let me come back out here and wait for them?" I asked, hoping to appease her.

"I can live with that."

I got up and followed Beth into the kitchen, only to find Jamie leaning against the counter, eating something out of a plastic container. There was a tense silence as I picked through the fridge to find the least objectionable choice. I looked at the sheet of instructions Gator left for warming it up before I put the container of pasta in the microwave.

"Drinking your dinner?" Jamie asked Beth as she poured herself a glass of wine.

"Cheers," Beth replied, holding her glass up in a mock toast.

I grabbed a fork out of the drawer, and my food after it came out of the microwave. I didn't have the energy to listen to them bicker. I pulled a blanket off of the couch on my way by, and resumed my vigil out on the porch, waiting for everyone to come home.

Rip's team got home first. He saw me on the porch and rode over so he could talk to me. "Have you been out here this whole time?" he asked, getting down off the horse.

"Basically," I replied. "Beth made me go inside to eat."

"Good. You don't eat enough, especially when you're nervous," Rip said. "And I can tell you're wound up tight tonight."

I pulled my blanket tighter around me as I stood up and walked to the rail. "Something doesn't feel right, Rip. I had the same feeling the day my mom died, but I just brushed it off. I know better now."

"They'll be fine. They all know what they're doing," he replied, trying to make me feel better.

"I hope I'm wrong," I sighed, feeling that pit in my stomach growing larger.

But I wasn't wrong...

Around midnight, Lee's team, including my father, came back to the ranch. I'd sat back down in my chair, and had dozed off while I was waiting.

The noise from the chopper landing near the house startled me awake. I pulled my blanket around me, as I got up and ran down the stairs to go meet my dad.

"Is everything okay?" I asked, meeting him halfway.

My dad squinted at me, "Everything's fine, why are you still up?" he asked.

"Where's Lee?" I asked.

"He's coming back with the group he left with," Dad replied. "Are you okay?"

"I just have a bad feeling that I can't shake," I mumbled. He walked me up to the porch, where I sat back down in my chair.

"Come inside, Charlotte," he said, opening the front door.

"I'm okay. I'm going to wait," I replied.

My head snapped around, when I heard the horses and trucks coming down the road. I stood up, and walked down to meet them as they rode past the house, toward the barn. My eyes raked over the returning men, searching for my brother, and not finding him.

I caught Ryan's eye, "Where's Lee?" I yelled, waving an arm.

He diverted from the group, and jumped down from the horse when he was close enough to bridge the gap. "We aren't sure, to be honest," he admitted, shaking his head.

One of the other cowboys, Lloyd, who I've known since I was a little girl, came over and joined the conversation. "We thought he was with us, when we left, but no one I've talked to on the ride back has seen him."

"No one's seen who?" Rip asked, coming back up to the house.

"Lee's missing. I told you this didn't feel right," I snapped. I broke away from the small group and ran up the steps to the house. "Dad!" I yelled, throwing the front door open.

"What, honey?" he asked, coming around the corner from the kitchen.

"He didn't come back with them. No one knows where he is," I told him.

"Fuck!" He pulled out his phone and tried to call Lee, to no avail.

"What is going on?" Jamie asked, sleepily coming downstairs. I'd clearly woken him up, because he was dressed for bed.

"We don't know where Lee is."

Within the hour, the yard was filled with people. Both my dad and Jamie were on the phone, trying to get different agencies to go out and look for Lee. I paced around the yard, praying that he'd come stumbling back home any minute.

On one lap around the yard, Ryan caught my eye, and nodded for me to follow him around to the other side of the house where we wouldn't be seen. I waited a few minutes, so that it wasn't that obvious.

It was darker on the other side of the house. It took a minute for my eyes to adjust and find Ryan in the darkness. "Over here," he said softly, stepping out of the shadows.

"Oh my god," I sighed, dropping my blanket, and rushing into Ryan's open arms. He held me as I started to shake. "I knew something was going to happen," I cried into his shirt.

"We'll find him, Charlie," Ryan said, quietly. "I promise." I felt him press his lips to my hair.

"I can't believe I just let him leave," I mumbled against Ryan's chest.

"You couldn't have known," he replied. I stepped back and looked up into his face, and Ryan wiped my tears away with his thumb. "What can I do to help you?"

I sniffed, and shook my head. "I don't know." I shifted my weight from one foot to another. "I feel sick to my stomach." I picked up my blanket and held it tight against my chest. "I just want to go back to happier times."

"I'd give anything to go back to the night we met," Ryan said. "Everything was perfect."

"I'd change one thing," I mumbled.

Ryan gave me a sad smile, "It worked out the way it was supposed to."

"Charlie?!" I heard Jamie call my name.

"Shit," I swore under my breath, and looked up at Ryan. "I have to go."

Ryan pulled me into his arms again. "I'm here if you need me." I always felt comfortable in his arms.

I walked back around to the front of the house, and found Jamie. "What?" I snapped at Jamie quietly as I rounded the corner of the house.

"You should go inside, and get some sleep," he told me.

"Fuck off," I mumbled. "There's no sleeping through this."

"At the very least, if you don't want to get caught with Ryan, stop wandering off in the same direction," Jamie said, leaning over to whisper in my ear.

"You are such a prick," I fumed quietly, and walked away.

At dawn, no one had heard from Lee, and no one had found him either. My dad had just told Jamie to call in the Feds when he spotted a rider in the field, headed toward the house. "It's Kayce," he said, looking through a pair of binoculars. I grabbed them to look for myself when he tried to hand them off to Jamie.

"He's got Lee," I said, handing the binoculars off to Jamie. "He's not moving."

Some of the horses were still tied up near the house. My father untied one, mounted it, and quickly ran off toward Kayce. I felt my knees start to buckle, and I grabbed onto Jamie to keep from falling.

Beth, who'd come outside in the early hours of the morning, grabbed onto me before Jamie could.

"I gotcha, Charlie. Let's go sit down," she said gently, leading me to sit on the steps as I started crying.

I leaned over against her shoulder, tears streaming down my face. "I shouldn't have fucking let him go," I sobbed, putting my head down.

"There was no stopping him, Charlie. Daddy said go, and Lee went," Beth said. Her eyes were dry, but the crack in her voice told me that she was just as upset about Lee as I was. "Here comes Kayce," she said.

I looked up, and Kayce was quickly approaching on the horse my dad had just left on. I stood up quickly, wobbling a bit, to go meet him. When he finally got off the horse, and I could properly look at him, he was a mess, covered in blood. "What happened?" I asked, reaching for him, trying to find the source of the blood.

"I'm fine. It's, it's not my blood," Kayce said.

"What happened, Kayce?" I pressed.

"I don't want to talk about it," he mumbled, looking away from me.

"That's not an option," Jamie said, from over my shoulder.

"Tell me the person who killed him is dead," I said, looking up into my twin brother's sad eyes.

"Yeah, he's dead, Charlie. You don't have to worry about that," Kayce confirmed.

I wrapped Kayce in a crushing hug, not caring about the blood getting on me. He hugged me back, and whispered, "We'll talk later. I need to talk to Monica first. I'll call."

"Okay," I nodded. I pulled back and wiped at my eyes.

"I'm goin' home," Kayce announced to Jamie and Beth.

"Not until you tell us what happened," Jamie snapped.

"There's nothin' to tell," Kayce replied.

After a tense standoff, Jamie called our chopper pilot, and had him take Kayce back home to the Reservation. Jamie, Beth, and I were left, staring at each other in tense silence. I was the first one to break the stare down, and looked out across the fields, to try to find my dad and Lee. I could see the horse near some trees, and could only kind of make out the outline of my dad sitting against the tree, with Lee in his lap.

I'm so tired of losing family members. First my mother, and now my oldest brother. Something has to change.

# Chapter 3

After a while, Jamie went inside, and just I stood in the yard, not knowing what to do. "Go clean up, Charlie, you're covered in blood from hugging him," Beth told me. "Come on, you can use my bathroom," she said, tugging at my arm.

To be honest, I think I was running on auto-pilot after that moment. When I came to, I was sitting in a hot bath, with no recollection of how I got there. I slid down under the water to get my hair wet. I was so emotionally drained of energy, but at the same time, I hated myself for not trying harder to stop him. Even if Beth was right, I still should have tried harder.

I scrubbed my skin raw, and got up out of the tub. I dried off with a towel that had been left on a nearby chair. I looked around for clean clothes to put on and swore under my breath. I really didn't want to have to make the trek over to the cabin in just a fucking towel.

"Charlie?" I heard Beth call as she tapped on the door. "I've got clothes for you. I went and got you some stuff so can stay for a couple days up here."

I felt myself deflate, and relax a bit. "Thank you," I replied.

"I'm gonna leave the bag on the bed, and you can come out and get changed," she told me.

"Okay." I waited to go out until I heard the bedroom door close. She'd packed a small duffel bag full of stuff for me. I dug my black sleep pants out from the bottom of the pile, and a green sweatshirt.

I changed and put my hair up into a wet bun, before walking out into the hall. Beth was leaning up against the wall. "I checked, your room is still in a livable condition, if you want to get some sleep," she suggested.

"I don't want to be by myself," I replied quietly.

"I'll lay in there with you, and if you happen to pass out on me, I won't hold it against you," she said. "You good with that?"

"Yeah," I nodded. We walked down the hall to my childhood bedroom. I pulled back the blankets and got under the covers, staring up at the ceiling. Beth got in next to me, and pulled the covers back up.

We laid there quietly for several long moments.

"Can I ask you a question?" she asked, looking over at me.

"Sure," I nodded slightly.

"Who did I see you with over on this side of the house last night?" Beth asked.

I felt my cheeks turning red. "His name is Ryan," I mumbled.

"That doesn't tell me who he is," she said, turning on her side to get a better look at me.

"He's one of the cowboys," I admitted.

"How long has this been going on?" she pressed. It became evident that she was trying to get me to think about something else.

"Um, about four months," I guessed. "He's a good guy, a real gentleman." I yawned and rolled over to face Beth. "What happened to What's-His-Face, that you were dating?" I asked, trying to change the subject.

"Got rid of him," she replied matter of factly.

"Why?" I yawned.

"He was a prick," Beth replied. The tone in her voice said that was all the information I was going to get on that subject. "So how did whatever this is with you and the cowboy start?"

"I met him at a bar before he started working here," I explained. "There's a little bit of a story," I said through another yawn. I rolled onto my side, and pulled the blankets tight around me. "I'll tell you later," I mumbled. "Daddy doesn't know."

Beth snorted, "You sure about that?"

"Mostly."

I fell asleep. I don't know when Beth got up, but when I woke up a few hours later, she was gone. I laid in bed for a bit, before going back downstairs.

The house seemed deserted, except for my dad. He was in his office with the door shut, but I could still hear him on the phone. I walked over and tapped on the glass door. He looked over, and waved me inside.

From the small bits of conversation that I heard, it sounded like he was making arrangements for Lee's funeral. I curled up in one of the big leather chairs in front of the desk.

"How are you holding up, sweetheart?" he asked when he hung up the phone.

"You and I both know I've had better days," I replied.

"Haven't we all?" he replied. "We're burying Lee in three days." He wasted no time sharing that information.

All I could do was nod my response.

"I want you to move back to the main house. I don't want you rattling around that cabin by yourself," he said.

Part of me wanted to protest, but the other part of me dreaded going back to the cabin, alone with all of Lee's things, like he'd be home any minute. "Fine. I'm going to need help getting my stuff up here."

"Take Colby in the morning."

"Okay."

I got up from the chair, and went back upstairs to find my boots. I grabbed my phone off the bed, and sent Ryan a text, asking if he could meet me at the cabin. I decided it was probably best if I did some packing.

Once I got my boots laced up, I made the trek over to the cabin that I shared with Lee. When I got to the cabin, I looked around, and Ryan wasn't there. I sat down on the porch, not quite ready to face it yet.

I looked up when I heard footsteps coming toward me, to find Ryan approaching, a little while later. "I'd ask how you're feeling, but I think I already know," Ryan said, sitting down on the step next to me. I leaned my head against his shoulder, as Ryan put an arm around me.

"I feel like crap," I mumbled, sniffing to hold back the tears.

"You don't have to hold it in, Charlie. It's okay to cry."

"I know," I replied as the tears started to fall. "My dad wants me to move back into the main house."

"Is that what you want?" he asked.

"Part of me does. I'm supposed to ask Colby to help me move my stuff in the morning. I came over to start packing, but I haven't gone inside yet."

"Do you want me to help?"

"I just don't want to be alone in there."

"Just tell me when you're ready."

I wiped my eyes and nodded. "Let's get this over with," I said, standing up. I stumbled a bit, and Ryan caught me as he stood up. "Thanks." I turned, walked up the stairs, and pushed open the front door.

Everything was where it had been left the day before. Our coffee cups were still sitting in the sink. Ryan trailed inside after me. "You can sit anywhere," I said.

I went back into my room, and pulled out my suitcases.

"Is there anything I can do to help?" Ryan asked again, following me into the bedroom.

"You're helping just by being here," I replied. "Just have a seat, and try to distract me while I work." I gesture to the chair in the corner of the room.

"How should I do that?" Ryan replied, raising an eyebrow at me. He took his hat off, and rested it on his knee as he sat down. "The only ways I can think of, aren't appropriate under the circumstances."

I couldn't help the giggle that escaped my lips. "How about you tell me a story?"

"What kind of story?"

"Surprise me."

(To be continued...)

# Chapter 4

(Note: The italics are supposed to be part of the story Ryan is telling Charlie. I just decided to do it this way to give a bigger picture of the night they met - that way it's not skewed to his perspective of the night he and Charlie met.)

~~~

I called Rip, hoping to catch him before he and the rest of the cowboys left for the bars. "What's the emergency, Charlie?" Rip asked, in lieu of a greeting.

"I heard Colby mention you guys are going to the bars tonight. Can I catch a ride?" I asked. My friends finally managed to talk me into going out on a Friday night.

"Only if you can get down to the bunkhouse in ten minutes," he replied.

"Done! Thank you!" I hung up the phone, put my boots on, and grabbed my hat before running out the door of the cabin. I made it over to the bunkhouse just as everyone was piling into the trucks.
~~~

"Just in time," Lloyd chuckled, beckoning me toward the truck he and Rip were in.

"Thanks!" I climbed in the backseat, and slid to the middle.

"I don't remember the last time you went to the bar," Rip teased. "Why tonight?"

I shrugged, "It's been a rough couple of weeks, and it's time to have some fun?"

"Sounds good to me."

When we got to the bar, I separated from the guys and went to go find my friends. I found them up near the stage, where the band was playing.

Over the course of the evening, I kept seeing this guy that was clearly new in town, because none of us had ever seen him before. We'd lock eyes, and flirt from across the room. Finally, as the night was winding down, and the band played a slow song, he came over to where I was, and held out his hand. "Will you dance with me?" he asked.

"Sure." I smiled and took his hand. "What's your name? I've never seen you in here before."

"Ryan. And what should I call you?"

"Charlotte," I replied.

He pulled me close, and wrapped an arm around my waist. I rested my free hand against his shoulder, and we swayed to the music. I'd be lying if I said he wasn't attractive, because he was very attractive. I'll always remember his eyes, and how kind they were. I didn't know him yet, but I could tell he was a good man.

"So what brings you to town?" I inquired, looking up into his blue eyes.

"Work," he answered. "I'm hoping to get hired on at one of the ranches."

"Good luck with that," I giggled. That had to be the alcohol talking.

"What about you? Are you from here?"

I nodded, "I am. I work on one of the ranches that are nearby."

"Which one?" Ryan asked.

I laughed, "Now where would be the fun in that?" I let him slowly spin me out and back into his chest. "It's more fun if I don't tell you, and we just see what happens."

He shook his head with a smile, "Why can't we do this the easy way?" Ryan asked.

"The easy way isn't fun," I pouted. "Why can't we have one fun, memorable night, and if it's meant to be, we'll meet again?" I suggested.

I could see him thinking it over, as we swayed to the music. "So, like serendipity?"

"Exactly."

"Okay."

The song ended, but we didn't part. The next song was a lot faster, so we picked up the pace a bit. He would spin me out quickly, and pull me back in to the point I was stumbling back into him and we would laugh. I would catch glimpses of my girlfriends watching us as we moved around the dancefloor.

When the song ended, the bartender called for last call. "Do you want another drink?" he asked.

Just as I was about to respond, I felt a hand on my shoulder, and I turned to find Rip standing right there. "If you're catching a ride with us, it's time to go."

I huffed, and rolled my eyes at him, "Fine. I need five minutes."

"Two."

I turned back to Ryan, "Please tell me that's not your boyfriend," he said.

I burst out laughing, "No! He might as well be my brother," I explained.

I watched Ryan visibly relax. "He seems grumpy," he laughed.

"You have no idea," I giggled. "But seriously, it's time to say goodnight."

"Then I better make this count." Ryan took my hat off and pushed my hair out of my face as he cupped my cheek and pulled me into a searing kiss. I kissed him back, standing up on my toes, and putting my arm around his neck to pull him closer.

We were both breathless when we pulled away. "Wow," I breathed. "I really hope I find you again," I said, taking my hat back.

"You could just give me your number," Ryan suggested.

"Serendipity," I replied, kissing him on the cheek.

"After a kiss like that, I want to hedge my bets," he said.

"I have a good feeling about you. If you come back into my life, I'll know I'm right." I replied. "Goodnight, Ryan." I turned and walked away, putting my hat back on.

On Monday morning, I was in the barn, putting new shoes on the horses, when someone came in. I didn't look up from what I was doing. My back was turned, and I couldn't see who it was. "I'm looking for Charlie. Do you know where I can find him?"

"You found her," I laughed, and stood up. The running joke on the ranch was to send the new hands looking for Charlie, and have them believe they were looking for a guy.

When I turned around, I froze. It was Ryan.

"Charlotte?" he asked.

"I mostly go by Charlie. My dad is really the only one who calls me by my full name," I explained. "I'm gonna blame the alcohol on why I told you to call me Charlotte," I laughed.

Ryan laughed with me, and his smile made me melt. "Well, does this mean I can get a real date?"

I nodded, "Yeah, but we have to keep this quiet."

"Why? Not supposed to date your co-workers?" he asked.

"I don't want to get you in trouble for messing with the farmer's daughter," I explained. "My full name is Charlotte Dutton."

"Wow," he replied, letting out a deep breath.

"If you don't want to keep this up, I understand."

"Who said I didn't want to keep this up? I'm not scared," Ryan said.

"Good," I smiled. "Now, what were you supposed to find me for?" I asked, getting back to business.

"They wanted me to bring this horse out when you're done," he replied.

"I've got one more shoe to put on, and then you can have her." I went back to work, and got the last shoe nailed into place. "She's all yours," I smiled, watching Ryan attach the lead rope to the bridle. "I'll catch you later."

"I look forward to it."

I smiled as Ryan recounted the story of how we'd met. "I wish I wasn't so stupid. I should have just given you my number. I'd be kicking myself if you didn't turn up again," I told him. "Serendipity is stupid - I got lucky you came back."

"To be fair, we were both a bit drunk," he teased as I fished my clothes out of drawers.

"Still." I packed my clothes down into the open suitcases.

I was satisfied with the progress I'd made while Ryan was telling me stories. There were only a couple more personal items to pack up in the morning. "We should probably be getting back," I frowned. We'd been in the cabin for over an hour, and surely someone was missing us - at least Ryan.

"One last thing, before we go." Ryan stood up and beckoned me into his open arms. He wrapped me in a hug, and I buried my face in his shirt, as I wrapped my arms around his torso. I treasure the stolen moments away from everyone. It's incredibly freeing to not have to care who's watching.

I backed up half a step, and leaned up to kiss him. The fireworks were still there from night one. Even in such a short, simple kiss, I could feel that familiar spark.

"Love you, Charlie," he sighed.

I looked up at him, wide-eyed. Neither of us had thrown the l-word out yet.

"I mean it. And if you're not ready to say it yet, that's fine. There's no pressure at all," Ryan said.

"I love you too," I replied with a small smile, feeling my face turn red. "But for real, you and I both know, Rip is looking for you. Go, before we get caught, and you get in trouble!"

"Really?" Ryan teased, "I tell you I love you, and you send me away?!"

"Only so you can live another day to tell me again," I replied, sticking my tongue out. "Love you!" I called as he was walking out the front door. I couldn't help the laugh that escaped my lips as I watched him hop the fence and run back toward the bunkhouse.

# Chapter 5

After Ryan left, I took my time cleaning up the kitchen, and looking to see what food needed to be used to keep it from going bad. Colby and I'd have to cart some of the food up to the house for Gator to use this week.

Knowing my time in the cabin was limited was sad. When I was done with my chores, I laid down on the couch and looked up at the rafters. Eventually, I heard my phone buzzing on the coffee table. I reached over and picked it up.

It was Kayce. "Hey, Kayce," I answered. "Are you okay?"

"Are you?" he replied.

"I've been better."

"Me too."

"What happened out there?" I asked.

There was a long pause before he responded to my question. "Usual deal? What we say stays between us?" Kayce asked.

"Duh," I replied.

"How much do you know about the cattle wandering onto the Reservation?"

"I knew that they were there, and still are there," I deadpanned. "That's about it."

"Well, Monica's brother was one of the people trying

to keep the cattle there," Kayce explained. I sensed where this was going, but I let him finish. "By the time I got there, Monica's brother shot Lee. I killed him before he could kill me, and to make him pay for what he did to Lee."

I took a deep breath to try to keep myself from crying. "Did Lee suffer? Don't bullshit me Kayce. I know when you're lying."

"If he did, it wasn't for long. The shot severed his spinal cord, so he wouldn't have felt much," Kayce replied. "Don't tell Dad or Jamie."

"I won't." I sniffed, wiping at my eyes as the tears started to fall. "I had the same feeling last night that I had the day Mom died. I tried to tell him it was a bad idea."

"You couldn't have known it was going to be him or anyone else, Charlie. Besides, Dad said go."

"Beth said the same thing."

"She's bound to be right every now and then," Kayce teased lightly. "Bottom line is, there's nothing you could have done to change what happened last night. So don't blame yourself."

Easier said than done. "Daddy said the funeral is in three days. You're coming, right?" I pressed.

There's a long pause. "I'll try, Charlie."

"Don't just try. Actually show up."

"We'll see."

We hung up a few minutes later and I continued staring up at the ceiling, trying to figure out what to do with myself. I didn't move for another thirty minutes or so. A knock on the door broke me out of my thoughts.

"Charlie, you in there?" It was Rip.

"It's not locked," I yelled, sitting up on the couch just as the front door swung open.

"Your dad said you've been gone awhile. He wanted me to come check on you," Rip said, leaning against the door frame.

"He told me to pack, so I did. I did some dishes." I stood up, pushing off the couch for support. "Does he think I'm going to do something stupid?"

"He wants you up at the house for dinner," Rip replied.

"Are we really doing a full dinner tonight?" I groaned.

"I don't think so, but he wants to make sure you eat something. Hell, you can join the cowboys for dinner as long as you actually eat something."

I shook my head, "I don't need to be a buzzkill for those guys."

"You need the company. You don't need to sit up here by yourself, blaming yourself for what happened," Rip replied. "I've known you long enough to know how you are," he said when I started to protest. "There was no way you could have stopped or changed what happened."

"Come on, let's go." He gestured for me to follow him outside after a long, silent pause.

"Fine. But I'm not hungry."

"You need to at least try."

We get down the stairs, and I see Rip's horse tied to the fence post. "I can walk back. I'll meet you there," I said.

"Bullshit," Rip smiled. "You're coming with me," he said as he untied the reins and got up into the saddle. "This is quicker than walking it." Rip offered me a hand.

I was being stubborn, but I took his hand and let him pull me up behind him. I wrapped my arms around him as he started to back up, so we could head toward the barn.

Rip has always been like another brother to me. I didn't care that he wasn't related to me by blood. Rip was family. I'm sure I was an irritation to him when I was growing up, but Rip was always kind, and infinitely patient with me when I tried to tag along while he was doing chores. Looking back, I think I probably made his chores take twice as long because I wanted to help.

My relationship with Rip was innocent. It was nothing like his relationship with Beth. I've known about whatever the hell was going on between them since before I left the ranch for school. I walked in on them once. I backed out quickly enough that neither noticed me.

"You're awfully quiet. What are you thinking about?" Rip asked. We were still a fair ways from the barn. There was no one else around.

"Nothing," I lied.

"We've known each other long enough to be honest," he said, looking back at me.

"Will you promise not to repeat it?" I asked.

"As long as you're not thinking about hurting yourself, Charlie," he replied matter of factly.

"I'm not." I shook my head. "I just wonder if the ranch is worth all of the death and fighting."

"You know he's fighting to hand it down to you and your siblings, right?" Rip asked, turning to look forward.

"I don't care about the ranch. I care about the people on it," I replied. "I don't want my Dad to work himself to death over land. It's not worth it."

"It's more than just the land, Charlie. It's the legacy."

"I'm glad someone understands him, because I don't."

Dinner was me standing in the kitchen poking at a piece of fish, while Beth watched. When she was satisfied, I went up to my room to be alone, and ended up passing out early.

# Chapter 6

Three days later, I woke up in my room in the main house. I had to force myself to get up, and get ready for Lee's funeral. It all just seemed so unreal to me. I put on a simple black dress, with a nicer pair of black ankle boots that I definitely don't wear for work.

There was a tap on my door as I was staring at myself in the mirror, trying to figure out what to do with my hair. "Come in," I said, barely loud enough to be heard.

The door was slowly pushed open, to reveal Beth on the other side. "How much longer are you going to be? You need to eat before we walk down there." Beth was wearing a suit with a white top underneath it.

I shrugged, "I don't know. I'm trying to decide if I should put my hair up or not."

"Leave it down. It's cute the way it is."

"Okay."

I decided not to really bother with much makeup because I would either sweat it off, or ruin it, crying. I followed Beth down to the kitchen so I could eat a quick something to appease my sister.

Gator was there when we entered. "What can I make you, Charlie?" he asked.

"Um, I'm probably just going to do a little bit of fruit, and coffee. Definitely coffee."

He gave me a sad smile, "I think I can manage that."

"Thank you."

My dad was the next one through the kitchen door, as I was making my coffee. "Have you heard from your brother?"

I knew better than to ask which one. He meant Kayce. "I talked to him a couple days ago," I replied. "I told him he needs to be here."

"Do you know if he's planning to show up, or not?" I think it came off harsher than he meant.

"I don't know," I mumbled.

Gator handed me a bowl of cut up strawberries, and I took it, and went to go sit at the dining room table. I sat down and forced myself to eat my breakfast. Jamie came in as I was getting up from the table.

"You look nice," he said, sitting down.

"You don't look too bad either," I replied. "I'm going to go sit outside. I think the fresh air will do me some good," I explained, gesturing to the window.

"Do you want company, or are you hoping to find it out there?" Jamie asked.

"You can do whatever you want, I just need to not be in here," I said, taking a deep breath. I exhaled as I turned to leave the house. The longer I stayed in the house, the more I felt like I was going to hyperventilate. I was already starting to feel dizzy.

Once I was outside, I started to feel better. I took a few more deep breaths and sat down on the front steps. "Are you okay, Charlie?" I look up to find Rip and Ryan standing in front of me.

"Yeah, I just needed the fresh air," I replied. "It was just really hot in the house."

"Did you eat?" Rip asked.

"Yes, Dad," I teased. "How's the new guy working out so far?" I asked, trying to change the conversation before Rip could get annoyed with me. I'd seen the new guy in passing over the last couple of days.

Ryan shrugged, "He's pretty new. Tough to say just yet." The fact that Ryan wearing a collared shirt, and a suit jacket was not lost on me. I wanted to say something, but I didn't want to say it in front of Rip.

I pushed off the stairs as cars start to roll up to the ranch. "Is it that time already?" I asked.

"I guess so. I'll let your dad know people are starting to show up," Rip said, heading up the stairs, and into the house.

Once it was just Ryan and I, I couldn't keep my comments to myself, but he beat me to it. "You look incredible, Charlie."

"I knew you cleaned up pretty well, but not this well," I smiled. The only thing I wanted to do was hug him, and not let go for a few minutes.

Colby, Lloyd, and the new guy wandered up and joined us, so any physical interaction would have to wait. "Morning," I sighed. "Beautiful morning, shitty circumstances, right?"

"You holdin' up okay?" Lloyd asked.

"As much as one can," I replied. "I'm Charlie," I said, turning to the new guy.

"Jimmy," he replied. "I'm sorry for your loss."

"Thank you." I turned back to the other three, "Would you guys ever consider letting me cook for the cowboys? I used to cook for me and Lee, and I miss it."

Lloyd chuckled, "You don't have to ask us twice! You can take Jake's night next week. He's horrible, so I'm sure your cooking will be better."

I smiled, "I'd really like that."

The rest of my family came outside as people continued to arrive. At eleven, the pastor directed us to follow him down to the graveside. I looked around for Kayce as we walked, but I couldn't find him. "He's not here," I mumbled to Beth.

"Of course not," she sighed.

Once we were at the graveside, I stood in between Jamie and Ryan. I looked around, and Rip, Lloyd, and my father were all standing far enough away, so I took Ryan's hand as we stood there, listening to the pastor talk. He squeezed my hand gently.

As we were leaving to go, Beth looped her arm through mine. "You're pretty reckless for someone not wanting to get caught."

"I honestly don't care right now," I replied. I stopped in my tracks when I saw Kayce, sitting in the grass on the walk back to the house. He was holding onto the lead rope of a gorgeous stallion that I'd never seen before. I was about to go talk to him, when Dad broke from the group to go talk to Kayce.

"I wouldn't, Charlie," Beth warned.

When we got back to the house, Jamie and Beth went to talk to some of the people who showed up for the funeral. I stood in the yard, and waited for Kayce, but he didn't come to the house. I saw my dad take the horse into the barn, but no sign of my twin brother.

"Meet me in the barn tonight? Eight-thirty?" Ryan asked, coming up to stand by me as I waited.

"Yeah, I can make that work," I nodded. "Love you," I whispered.

"Love you too."

My father came up to the house as the last people were leaving. "Where's Kayce?" I asked.

"He didn't stay," my dad snapped. "Come here," he gestured to Beth and Jamie to join us. "I need you three now, more than ever. Are you with me?"

"Yeah," Jamie and I said together.

"Of course," Beth said. "I'll stay as long as you need me to stay."

"Good, because it's about to get difficult." I honestly didn't know how it could get more difficult than a dead sibling, and a big part of me did not want to know.

...

Around 8:20 that night, I put on some boots, and headed for the front door, hoping to not get caught. "Where are you headed?" My father asked, looking at me over his shoulder from his place on the couch.

"Nowhere. I just want some fresh air. I thought I might go look at the horse Kayce left," I replied.

"Just be careful," he said as I walked out the front door.

The barn was empty when I got there. I was genuinely curious about the horse, so I walked over to the stall and opened the top half of the gate so I could get a better look.

The horse turned to face me as I opened the gate. "You're very handsome," I smiled, offering my hand. He wasn't interested in me quite yet. The horse snorted and turned away from me.

"You're pretty cute too," Ryan said, coming to stand in front of the stall. "How are you holding up?"

"Better, now." I turned and wrapped my arms around him, burying my face in his chest. He held me close, and I just felt safe. After a few long moments, I took half a step back so I could lean up to kiss him for the first time in days.

Ryan and I turned to look at the horse. He had an arm wrapped around my waist, as I leaned into him. "You ruined the joke for Jimmy," he teased.

"Hmmm?" I raised an eyebrow.

"Where we get to make him think you're a guy," he clarified.

I chuckled, "He didn't look like he could take it. He looked like the type of keel over from shock. I can't have that on my conscience."

"Did you know he's branded?" Ryan asked, looking down at me.

"No. I thought Rip and Lloyd were the only ones." I shook my head gently. I reached my hand into the stall to try to get the horse's attention.

"It's fresh."

"Wow." Part of me wondered what the story was there. "I don't think he likes me very much."

"Jimmy?"

"The horse," I giggled.

"Let's see how far bribery gets you." Ryan pulled an apple out of the pocket of his sweatshirt, and his pocket knife. He cut the apple up into pieces, and handed me a couple.

I made a noise to get him to look back in my direction. His ears perked up, seeing the apple piece in my hand. Finally, he turned fully around to face us. I laid one of the pieces on my flat palm, and offered it to the horse. He sniffed my hand for a moment, before deciding to take the apple.

"So bribery will get me somewhere," I smiled. I fed him my second piece, as Ryan cut more up. "Do you have plans next Friday?" I asked, looking over at Ryan.

"Not that I'm aware of. Why?"

"Want to go sneak off and go to the bars? One of my favorite bands is playing."

"As long as we're done working at a decent hour, I think I can make that work," he smiles, feeding the horse himself. "Is your brother okay? He looked pretty broken up earlier."

"Kayce?" I confirmed. "I don't know. I wish he'd have stayed. I can usually get a good read on where he's at in about five minutes. I know he feels guilty."

"That's understandable,"Ryan nodded.

"It is. I just wish I could take some of that pain from him, or make him remember he's not in this alone."

"Give it time. That's about the only thing you can do. Did he tell you what happened?"

I nodded, "But he invoked Twin Code, so I can't repeat it."

"Even if it would help him some way?" he asked.

"When Twin Code is invoked, nothing is repeated - but I can badger him to divulge if I know it's in his best interest to come clean," I explained. "Most of the time he listens to me."

"My siblings and I would sell each other out in a heartbeat when we were kids. Like, this one time, we were playing baseball in house, after we'd been told not to a million times. We thought we were good enough to keep it contained. I threw a ball, and my brother knocked it into the next room, and broke my mom's antique clock. My sister told my mom everything the second she ran into the room."

I laughed, "That was Jamie, growing up. So how much trouble did you get into?"

"Oh we were grounded for at least a month on that one."

"I'm the baby of the family, so I only got in trouble when I really screwed up." Ryan gave me a couple more apple pieces, and I fed them to the horse.

"Yeah, that was not my experience growing up." He let out a wry laugh.

"I'm usually the one trying to make and keep the peace, so no one really threw me under the bus," I shrugged.

"Last one," Ryan handed me the last piece of apple. "I think you're at least starting to make friends."

"Me too." I fed my last piece to the horse, and when he was done he nuzzled against my empty palm. When he was done, I pulled my hand away, and closed the gate.

I can't stifle the yawn that escapes my lips. "I think it's time for bed," Ryan said.

"You're probably right."

He leaned down and kissed me, pushing my hair back. I couldn't help but smile into the kiss, as I deepened it by pulling him closer. We were both out of breath when we pulled away. He took my hand and led me out of the barn, where we ran straight into Rip...

# Chapter 7

"What are you two doing out here this time of night?" Rip asked, almost glaring at us. Ryan, to his credit, did not drop my hand.

"I wanted to see Kayce's horse," I replied.

"And you?" Rip turned to Ryan.

"I was headed back to the bunkhouse when I saw her come in. I just wanted to make sure she didn't need help," Ryan said.

"Charlie, I'm not stupid," Rip said, letting out a wry chuckle. "I know you've been sneaking around. I remembered him from the bar right before he started here."

Ryan and I glanced at each other quickly before turning back to Rip. "Does everyone know?" I asked, tightening my grip on Ryan's hand.

"All the cowboys know, except maybe Jimmy. I know Lee knew. To my knowledge, your father doesn't know," Rip explained.

"Does he really have to?" I asked.

"Only if this becomes a problem." He gestured between the two of us.

"I'm not going to cause any problems," Ryan replied. "We're both adults."

"No one means to cause problems. Sometimes, shit happens. Just know, I might call on you for some extra help around the ranch," Rip smiled.

It didn't seem like Rip knew how much I was aware of his relationship with Beth, and I wasn't about to let him abuse Ryan. "Seems like a little bit of a double standard, Rip." I raised an eyebrow at him.

"What do you mean, Charlie?" he asked.

"I think we should continue this conversation, just the two of us," I replied, not wanting to out his secret, even though he held mine in the palm of his hand.

"Alright, Ryan, head back to the bunkhouse," Rip nodded.

"It's okay," I replied when Ryan looked to me for confirmation.

"I'll see you in the morning," he nodded, squeezing my hand, before leaving us.

"What are you going on about?" Rip asked when we were alone.

"I've known about you and Beth for well over a decade, and I've kept my mouth shut. I would never do that to either of you. Is it too much to ask for the same amount of respect?" I asked, crossing my arms over my chest.

Rip closed his eyes and let out a long frustrated sigh before looking back down at me. "Does he make you happy?"

"Very. He's a good man, Rip. Give him a chance, and don't abuse him."

"I'll give him a chance for you, but if he hurts you, I will handle that problem my way," Rip warned. "And you have to keep it professional while others are around, or your father will figure it out."

"We're not stupid either," I smiled. "Lee admitted that he knew about us. He gave me shit for catching us in the barn about a week or so ago."

"You aren't subtle at all," Rip teased as we walked back to the house.

"Neither are you!"

He laughed, and gently pushed me toward the house. "Go to bed. We've got an early start in the morning."

"When don't we?" I asked, heading up the stairs. I pushed open the front door. The living room was empty, and I didn't meet anyone on my way to my room. I changed, and got settled into my bed. I sent Ryan a message that he didn't have anything to worry about.

...

The next morning, I started my day, checking on some of our cows that were pregnant, and could go into labor any day now. They all checked out and were doing fine. When I was done, I headed back to the barn so I could grab my horse.

I didn't make it to the barn, because I got distracted by the sight of Rip and my dad taping Jimmy to Kayce's horse in one of the pins nearby. There was a small crowd assembled. "Dare I ask what the hell this is?" I asked, leaning on the fence by Colby.

"Jimmy is going to help break this horse in," Rip replied.

"How do we expect this to go?" I asked, looking down the line at Ryan.

"Not well," Ryan laughed, three people away from me.

"Who's your money on?" Colby asked. "Jimmy or the horse?"

"Can I just put my money on him puking before the day is over?" I ask.

"How much?"

"$20."

"Deal."

Once Rip and my dad were out of the pin, Jimmy was ordered to kick the horse. When he did, the horse seemed to come to life, trying to buck him off. But for the duct tape, Jimmy would have been on the ground in seconds.

"Good god," I shook my head, watching the horse try to buck Jimmy off. "He's in for a rough day."

Colby and Ryan chuckled, and Ryan made a comment that he was happy not to be Low Man anymore. I couldn't say I blamed him, watching what Jimmy was going through.

I stepped back from the fence, and turned back to the barn. "What? You're not gonna stay for the show?" Colby called.

I turned back to face him, "I'll be back later to see how they're doing! I have other things to do today!"

I was in the barn alone for a few minutes before Ryan came in, "Am I allowed to ask what you said to Rip after I left last night?" he asked, watching me saddle my horse.

"His secret isn't mine to tell," I replied, "But he'll keep our secret. Do you trust me?"

Ryan nodded, "I trust you. I'm not sure how much I trust Rip."

I stopped what I was doing, and moved to stand in front of Ryan, and took his hands. "He's like my brother. He's not going to say anything. I trust Rip with my life."

I watch Ryan relax, "I'll trust him as long as you do."

"Thank you."

He pulled me in and kissed me deeply, dropping my hands, to wrap his arms around my waist. This feels so wrong, because we could get caught at any moment, but that's also what makes it so thrilling.

I stepped back, out of breath, and smiling like an idiot. "I gotta go start my rounds, otherwise I'll be gone all day."

"I love you, Charlie."

"I love you too."

...

I was out, doing my rounds when my phone rang. I pulled it out, and saw that it was Jamie. That was odd. He never called in the middle of the day. "Hey, what's up?" I answered.

"I need some advice. Beth was no help, as usual," he sighed.

"What's wrong?" I asked. He only ever asked for advice if something was wrong.

"What did Kayce tell you? I know you talked to him, Charlie."

"No I didn't," I lied.

Jamie sighed again, clearly frustrated. "Fine, let me tell you what the Governor, the Attorney General, and I know! He shot that guy in the forehead while he laid on the ground, bleeding out."

"That guy was Monica's brother," I mumbled.

"Jesus Christ," Jamie fumed. "Do you have any advice on how to deliver this lovely message to our father?"

"I'd just rip the band aid off. He'd rather you be straight with him," I replied.

"Wish me luck, I have to tell him that he's going to have to exhume Lee, and have him cremated. If he says anything to you about it, I need you to back me up! It's the only way we keep Kayce out of prison!" Jamie said. "This only works if you're on my side, because God knows I can't trust Beth."

I took a deep breath and looked up to the sky, trying to keep myself from crying. "What happens with Lee's ashes after the fact?"

"That's not my problem right now," he replied.

"I told you what I think. I will support you if I'm asked my opinion on the subject. Is that all you need?" I asked, trying to do my best to not snap.

"Yes. I'm sorry, Charlie." His voice was softer.

"Yep." I hung up the phone and went on with my day.

By the time I made it back to the barn, Jimmy was still riding around the pin. "How's he doing?" I asked, walking over to Rip, who was sitting on the gate.

"He's still up there," Rip nodded.

"Has he puked yet? That's what I put my money on," I smiled.

"Not yet."

My dad came over to the pin and told Rip to let Jimmy down. Rip climbed into the pin, and stepped in the horse's path, causing him to stop. Rip cut the tape, letting Jimmy down. He stumbled, and held onto the gate for balance as Rip got up on the horse, who was now much easier to ride.

"How do you feel, Jimmy?" I asked, moving to stand in front of him.

He gave me a weak thumbs up, but he looked nauseous. Rip climbed down from the horse and told Jimmy to take him back to the barn, wash him down, and not to feed him until he'd cooled off. On the way back to the barn, I saw Jimmy stop, and bend over at the waist to throw up.

"Maybe he's got some cowboy in him after all," my father commented.

I chuckled, "He just made me some money."

...

I was headed up to bed later that night, when my dad called me into his office. "Have a seat, Charlotte," he pointed to the chair across the desk. I felt like I'd been called into the principal's office. "Jamie told me that you know what happened that night. Kayce told you."

"I don't know where Jamie got that idea," I replied with a straight face.

"Bullshit! I know you talk about everything. You told Jamie that Kayce killed Monica's brother. We didn't know that. Why deny it?"

"Kayce asked me not to say anything. I thought Jamie knew that already," I replied.

"I hate that you two keep secrets."

"It's what twins do."

"What are your thoughts on cremation?" The change of topic threw me for a moment.

"I don't think it's a bad thing. If it's going to keep Kayce safe, isn't that what's important?"

"So you've talked to Jamie too?" My father let out a wry laugh.

"Technically, he called me. I think he's right, though. This is how we protect Kayce." I pause for a beat. "What will you do with Lee's ashes?"

"Do you have any suggestions?" He asked.

"No," I shook my head. "Can I be there when you do it?"

"Why?"

"So I can say goodbye one last time."

My father sighs and reluctantly agrees. After that, he dismissed me, and I went up to my room.

Before turning in for the night, I texted Kayce to tell him that we needed to talk. It's urgent. I got a response telling me that I could come down to the Reservation so we could talk, and so I could see Tate. He mentioned something about Tate wanting to show me something.

# Chapter 8

The next day, my schedule was lighter, so I got all my stuff done on the ranch, and headed down to go see Kayce and Tate.

When I got there, Tate was running toward my car before I even came to a full stop. He hugged me the second I was out of the vehicle, "Charlie!! You have to see it!!"

"Have to see what? Your dad said he wasn't going to ruin the surprise," I told him, as Tate dragged me by the hand to a hole in the ground.

"My dinosaur!"

"What?" I asked, looking down into the hole. "Holy shit," I mumbled, realizing that I was looking at a huge dinosaur skeleton. "How did you find it?"

"Dad blew up the tractor!"

"What?" I turned to look at my brother, who had followed us over to the hole.

"I'll explain in a minute. Buddy, you need to go inside while we talk. You can come back when we're done," Kayce told Tate.

Tate huffed, but did what he was told.

"Start with the tractor, then we can get into what I came here for," I told him. I was too interested in that story to start with my own.

"It's not that exciting. There was a rock that I was using the tractor to pull up. The tractor flipped. I loosened it up with some nitro..."

I couldn't help but laugh. "I bet Monica loved that."

"I'm so far in the dog house, it's not funny. What was so urgent?"

"The Governor and the Attorney General know there was a third shooter. No one knows it was you, yet. Dad and Jaime are doing what they can to keep you out of it."

"Fuck," he sighed, shaking his head. "What was I supposed to do?"

"You did exactly what you were supposed to do, Kayce. I'm telling you what I know. Dad's going to have Lee exhumed and cremated. God only knows what else he's going to do."

Kayce rubbed his eyes and shook his head.

"Just let him help you. You know Mom would want him to help you."

"Wow, you're pulling the "Mom" card?" he asked, turning back to face me.

"Yeah, I am! Just don't make this harder for him than it has to be."

"Fine." He paused for a moment, before continuing. "Maybe I really should just go back to the Navy, and solve everyone's problems?"

"How the hell does that solve anyone's problems?" I asked.

"I can't provide for my family just training horses."

"No, you're just trying to run from your problems," I shot back.

"You sound like Monica."

"Then maybe we're right!" I paused, and took a moment to relax. "Please, Kayce. I feel like I just got you back. Don't go away again." I took a deep breath, trying not to cry.

"Come here, Charlie. Don't cry." Kayce pulled me into a hug and I dissolved into tears as I wrapped my arms around my brother. "Please don't cry."

"I can't lose another brother."

He sighed, "Alright. I won't go."

"Thank you," I sniffed.

...

When I got home, Jaime met me at the porch. "I know you went to see him."

"So what?"

"What did you tell him?" Jaime pressed.

"I told him not to make this harder than it's going to be. You and I both know, he can be a stubborn pain in the ass." I crossed my arms over my chest. "I did what I could to soften him up, but you know how he is."

Jaime lets out an exasperated sigh. "Well, you were more help than Beth." He softened a bit, "I appreciate you trying." He paused for a moment before changing topic, "I'm supposed to tell you that we're exhuming Lee tonight. Dad said that it's probably best that you don't go."

"Why?" I snapped.

"Dad said he thought about it, and he doesn't want too many witnesses. He's trying to protect you, Charlie. This way, if anyone ever finds out, you don't have to get up in court and testify that we dug Lee up, and cremated him to protect Kayce."

I saw red, "Are you fucking kidding me, Jamie?"

"I'm sorry."

"Whatever."

"I know you don't like the decision, or understand it, but it's for the best."

"Fuck you."

"It'll be okay, Charlie," Jamie responded softly.

"How do you know?" I snapped.

"I wouldn't tell you it was going to be okay if I thought it wasn't. You know I wouldn't bullshit you like that," Jaime replied.

"Promise?"

"Have I ever done that to you before?"

"No." But there's a first time for everything. Why else does Beth hate him so much?

I avoided family dinner that night, because I couldn't look my dad or Jamie in the face just yet. I stayed out in the fields, and skipped dinner altogether. After it got dark, and I knew Jamie and my dad were gone, I grabbed a bottle of tequila out of the kitchen and walked back to my cabin, and sat down on the porch. I texted Ryan, on the off chance he hadn't gone to bed already.

C: Are you busy?

I waited about ten minutes, and I thought I was going to be drinking alone, but he texted me back.

R: Nope. Just got out of the shower. What's up?

C: Bad day, and tomorrow isn't looking much better. I just wanted some company.

R: I can do that. Where are you?

C: My cabin.

R: Headed your way now.

By the time Ryan made it to me, I'd had several shots, and given that I was drinking on an empty stomach, I was already pretty tipsy. He sat down next to me on the step, and I tried to pass him the bottle. "You're behind a few shots," I giggled.

"How do you drink this without a lime?" he asked, looking over at me.

"Practice," I replied. Beth taught me when I was probably a little bit too young. He pushed the bottle back, and so I just took another shot.

"What happened, Charlie? I've never seen you do this."

I leaned over, putting my cheek against his arm, as I put the bottle down in between our feet. "I have one brother currently being exhumed and cremated, another that's trying to run away back to the military, and tomorrow is the anniversary of the day my mom died. This family is a fucking mess."

Ryan moved the bottle away, and moved closer, putting his arm around me. "I'm sorry. It-"

"Don't tell me it's going to be okay. Jamie tried to give me that bullshit. He can't know if all of this crap will turn out to be okay. No one can." I was definitely drunk, and things were spinning slightly.

"I was just going to say that it sounds like you're going through a lot right right now, and I don't know what to say," he replied quietly.

"Sorry," I sniffed, inhaling the scent of his cologne and soap. "You smell really good," I mumbled.

He chuckled, and rubbed my back. "I told you I just got out of the shower."

"My point still stands," I replied, taking a deep breah. "Can we just stay here tonight?"

"I can stay for a little while, but I can't stay all night," he told me.

"I can live with that," I yawned. I stumbled to my feet, and caught myself on the railing. Ryan stood up effortlessly, and helped me back up the stairs. He opened the door to the cabin, and I walked inside, turning on the light.

I used the couch to balance as I walked back to my room. Ryan followed me, closing the front door behind himself. He also turned off of the light in the living room once I made it into my room, and got the light on.

At the very least, my bed was still made up. I pulled the covers back before I slipped out of my jeans and boots and laid down on the bed. "Come here," I said, patting the mattress next to me.

"Not to state the obvious, but you're drunk, and I'm not going to do something that we're both going to regret in the morning," Ryan said, pulling my blanket up to my chin.

"I'm not asking you to sleep with me. I just want you to lay here with me," I yawned.

"I can live with that," Ryan said, smiling down at me. He turned out the light and laid down next to me, on top of the covers. I cuddled into him, and closed my eyes.

"Thank you," I mumbled into his shoulder.

"I've got your back, Charlie, and occasionally, your hair. I'm not going to tell you it's all going to be okay, but I will tell you that I know you'll make it through whatever is thrown your way," He told me. "You're stronger than you know."

"You're too good to me," I yawned.

# Chapter 9

When I woke up the next morning, I was alone in bed with a splitting headache. I rolled over and found a glass of water and painkillers on the nightstand. "You really are too good to me," I yawned, taking a couple of the pills.

I laid there for a few more minutes and let the pills start to do their work. When I was finally able to get up without the world spinning, it was later in the morning than I'd meant to sleep through. I got up and got dressed before making the slow, miserable trek back to the main house.

When I got there, Beth was naked, sitting in a trough, and drinking straight from a bottle of champagne. "If you're gonna give me a lecture too, you can save it," she called as I approached.

"No," I shook my head. "I know what today is. I was just going to ask for a sip," I said, nodding at the bottle. "I have such a hangover that I'm willing to see if this helps."

"Knock yourself out," Beth replied, handing me the bottle. "I missed you at dinner last night."

"I don't want to talk about it yet," I said just before putting the bottle to my lips. I tipped my head back and took a good sized gulp. "Thanks." I handed the bottle back and headed inside.

On my way up to my room, I met the Governor of Montana as she slipped out of my dad's room. I wish I could say that was shocking on some level. I was probably numb to it by that point, if we're being honest. Or maybe I was too hungover at the moment to care?

"Morning, Governor," I yawned, not really stopping for pleasantries.

"Charlotte," she nodded, and kept moving.

Before I made it back to my room, Jaime came up the backstairs and stopped me. "Where have you been?" he asked quietly.

"My cabin," I replied.

"You smell like tequila," he said.

"Well, I did get drunk on tequila last night. Now I'm going to go shower and figure out what to do with my day," I explained.

"You were missed at dinner last night," Jamie said.

"I don't really care. It's not like there will never be another family dinner. Besides, it's not like Beth sticks around through the whole meal."

"You're going to have to face him at some point, Charlie. You can't avoid Dad forever," he pointed out.

"Watch me." I pushed past Jamie into my bedroom, shutting and locking the door behind me. I pulled out my phone when I felt it buzz.

R: How do you feel this morning?

C: My head is killing me. It's a wonder I haven't thrown up.

R: Lots of water, and take it easy today!!

C: I think I want to move back into the cabin. I can't stay here.

R: I'll tell Colby he gets to move all your stuff back ;)

C: Most of it is still packed up. I'll load up an ATV and do it myself if I have to.

R: At the risk of admitting to seeing something I shouldn't have, is your sister okay?

C: Today is harder for her than the rest of us, for good reason. So if that's the worst she's going to do, so be it. No judgment from me.

R: Is there anything I can do?

C: Just give me a hug later.

R: I can do that.

The day my mom died, we were branding cows. Beth, Kayce, and I were given the option to go for a ride with my mom, or learn how to brand calves. Beth and Kayce chose the former; I went with the latter.

My dad saw the horses coming back to the barn without my mom or Kayce. That was the first clue that something was very wrong...

Beth and Kayce have never really told me a lot about what happened that morning, but I'd gotten the gist of it. Beth has gotten a lot of shit over the years, for our mom's death. I've tried not to contribute to that, but I know I have said some cruel things when we fought over the years.

I took a shower and dressed for the day before going downstairs to have some coffee and toast around 10am. Once I was done, and confident that nothing was going to come back up, I went down to the corral.

When I got there, Rip was having the cowboys practice roping. Lloyd was driving the ATV that was pulling the dummy around.

"Charlie, go get a horse and get out here!" Rip called as I leaned against the fence to watch.

"Are you sure?" I asked.

"Yes! Let's go!"

I turned and walked quickly back to the barn to saddle my horse, and get my rope. Once I was ready, I rode back to the corral, where Jimmy opened the gate to let me in.

Rip had Jimmy and I take a round together. To say it wasn't my best work was an understatement. "Again, Charlie. You're better than that."

"Yep. I just need some time to warm up," I replied. Warm up took about three more rounds before I stopped sucking. I suspected that Rip told them to take it easy on me, because normally Colby and Lloyd would have been giving me crap after one bad round.

I finally caught a break, and I was watching Jimmy and Fred go. I noticed a bunch of cars drive past on the way up to the house. "Wonder what that's about," I said, nodding in that direction to Ryan, who just shrugged. "It might be enough coverage to load my luggage down the backstairs onto an ATV or two," I mumbled.

"Are we really moving your stuff back?" Colby asked.

"I can do it. My stuff was never really unpacked."

"We can help," Ryan offered.

Thirty minutes later, we had three ATVs pulled up to the back of the house. I had three suitcases and two duffel bugs full of stuff that had to go back to the cabin. We moved as quietly as we could up the backstairs. With three people, it only took one trip.

"I'm not doing this again," Colby said, as we strapped the luggage to the ATVs.

"I'm hoping I don't have to do this again either," I replied.

We got all of my stuff into the cabin, and drove the ATVs back to where they're stored. "You said you wanted to cook for the cowboys sometime," Colby said.

"I did."

"You can take my turn tomorrow."

"Please do," Ryan cut in.

I laughed, "Sure. I'll make dinner tomorrow."

"I'm headed back to the bunkhouse, so you can have your alone time now," Colby teased lightly.

"We have to get him a girl," I giggled when he was gone.

We stepped into the shadows on the other side of the barn. I leaned up against the wall, and let out a deep breath. It was a quiet, cool night. It felt good to steal another moment.

He moved to stand in front of me. "Are you okay?" Ryan asked, brushing my hair back out of my face. He let one hand rest on my waist, and I rested mine against his chest.

I nodded, "Yeah. This is always a rough time of year. Losing Lee just made it worse. Thank you for taking care of me last night."

Ryan smiled, and leaned in to kiss me on the forehead. He rested his forehead against mine as I leaned up to kiss him. Just as my lips touched his, I heard something hard hit the floor of the barn, and Beth start speaking. I jumped, hitting Ryan in the face.

"Ow!" He backed away, holding his nose.

"I'm so sorry!" I whispered. "Are you okay?"

He pulled his hand away, and I used the light from my phone to see if he was bleeding. "No blood," he breathed.

"We should get some ice on that anyway," I replied. We were about to move away when we heard Jamie start yelling at Beth. As we passed the door of the barn, Beth hit Jamie, and before I could react, Jamie punched Beth, knocking her to the ground.

"What the fuck is wrong with you two?" I snapped, walking into the barn, Ryan on my heels.

"Stay out of this, Charlie," Beth said, standing up.

"Let me look," I said, trying to gauge the damage. "You need to ice your cheek."

Jamie looked over my shoulder at Ryan, "Are you sure you really want to join this family?"

"Shut up. You've said more than enough." I stepped toward him, jabbing him hard in the ribs. "You can clean that cut yourself." I turned on my heel and stomped out of the barn.

Ryan followed me out, and I stopped a fair distance away from the barn. "I'm so sorry," I said, turning to look at him. "I don't know what the hell is wrong with them. They've always fought like cats and dogs, but the physical violence is new." I paused only to take a breath, "Is your nose okay?"

"I'm fine, Charlie. You have nothing to apologize for." He leaned down and kissed me softly. "I think it's time to call it a night."

"I think you're right," I nodded.

"You've got a gun, right? I don't like thinking of you sleeping out there alone with no protection," Ryan explained.

"Oh, yeah. There's a rifle over the front door, and I have a pistol in the nightstand - not to mention my stun gun," I replied. Part of me wanted to suggest that he could always sleep out at the cabin if he wanted to, but after nearly breaking his nose, and Jamie, it seemed like a bad idea.

"Good," he smiled down at me.

I leaned up and kissed him goodnight. "Love you," I whispered.

"Love you more."

# Chapter 10

I started the trek back to the cabin, using the light on my phone to see. When I got there, my dad was sitting on the porch in one of the rocking chairs. "Did you really think no one noticed you, Colby, and Ryan sneaking down the backstairs with your stuff?" he asked, gesturing for me to sit down.

"I was mostly hoping that they would keep their mouth shut. So, who ratted me out?" I asked, preferring to stand. I crossed my arms over my chest.

"Doesn't matter. Why are you avoiding me all of the sudden?"

"Why did you go back on your word?" I responded. "Better yet, why did you let Jamie tell me?"

My dad nodded silently. "I know you don't believe that I was trying to protect you, but I was. As for Jamie telling you, I was going to tell you, but he got to you first."

"Speaking of Brother Dearest, what the fuck is with him and Beth?"

My dad chuckled, "You have a better chance at pulling that information out of them than I do."

"Well, they've progressed to physical violence," I shrugged.

"Jesus Christ," he swore under his breath.

"Yeah. Maybe it is best that we don't all live under one roof."

"I don't like the idea of you out here alone," he replied, shaking his head.

"I have a rifle, pistol, and a couple stun guns in here. I'll be fine," I explained.

"I don't doubt that," he chuckled. "Maybe bring a couple of the dogs with you?"

"We'll see," I conceded.

"How bad was it?" Dad asked, changing the topic back to Beth and Jamie.

I finally sat down in the other chair. "Oh, you'll be able to tell when you see them. Jamie's ribs might be a little sore for a couple days too." I admitted.

He shook his head. "Maybe you're right. A little distance isn't a bad thing." He got up from the chair and pulled me up into a hug. "I'm serious about the dogs."

"Not tonight. I'm not making the trek back to the barn and back again tonight," I protested.

"Tomorrow, then." He let me go, and headed back for the main house.

I went inside and locked the door. Just to appease everyone, I checked all the windows to make sure they were locked before crawling into bed and passing out.

...

I was relieved to see that Ryan's face wasn't bruised when I saw him the next day. I told him about my dad showing up at the cabin last night. "He wants me to take a couple of the dogs with me tonight," I explained.

"See, I'm not the only one that worries about you being alone that far out," Ryan smiled, feeling vindicated.

"Yes, you win," I said, shaking my head.

My day was fairly quiet. Early that morning the cattle from the Reservation had been dropped off at the ranch, so we had to separate them out by owner and get them onto their respective trailers. That took up a good chunk of the day.

I cut out a bit early, to go feed the dogs, and start on dinner for the cowboys. I'd chosen to make a big pot of chili with cornbread.

"I thought it was Colby's night to cook?" Rip asked, coming up while I was dumping my ingredients into the pot on the fire.

"I volunteered to take his night," I replied.

"That's probably for the best. I swear I had food poisoning the last time he cooked," he chuckled.

"Ryan sounded like it was better that I take over," I commented, stirring everything together.

"Have you seen Ryan and Colby?" Rip asked.

"Um, I think I saw them walk around the barn, but I don't know how long ago that was. They were with Jimmy and Fred."

"Thanks."

I didn't think anything of it until Jimmy showed up to dinner bloodied, and Fred didn't show at all. Jimmy filed through the line, and tried to keep his head down. "What happened to your face?" I pressed.

"Nothing, it's fine," he replied.

"Jimmy, I don't give a shit about the no fighting rule. You're not in trouble. I just want to make sure you're okay," I told him.

"I'm okay, Charlie," he replied. "Just hungry."

"Sure." I ladled several large scoops of chili into his bowl. "If you need help cleaning that later, let me know."

"Thank you."

Ryan and Colby sauntered over after Jimmy moved away. "Is he okay?" Colby asked.

"What happened?" I pressed.

"Fred," Ryan replied. "Jimmy wouldn't stay down."

"Good for him, for standing up to that prick," I replied quietly as I scooped chili into their bowls. "He's the reason I always carry a stun gun on me."

Ryan's head snapped up, "What did he do?"

"Just some comments that never sat right with me," I replied. "He caught me out late one night when I was headed back to the cabin and made several comments that made me uncomfortable."

"Why didn't you ever say anything?" Ryan asked quietly.

"Rip would have him sent away instantly," Colby chimed in.

I shook my head. "He ceased to be an issue after I used the stun gun on him that night," I explained.

They stared at me in shock.

"This was before either of you started working here. That's why I didn't bring it up."

"Jesus, Charlie, I had no idea," Ryan said, still trying to stay quiet.

"I promise, the next time I get harassed, I'll let you both know."

"And Rip."

"'And Rip' what?" Rip asked, appearing behind them.

"It's nothing," I replied. "We can talk about it later."

"I'll hold you to that."

I served Rip his dinner before getting a bowl for myself. I took my dinner and went to sit with the guys while we ate. I received several compliments on my cooking, and I was told in no uncertain terms that I was welcome to cook dinner whenever I felt like it.

After dinner, Rip made Colby and Ryan do the cleaning up, so I didn't have to. Rip walked me back to the barn, to get a couple of the dogs before I went back to my cabin.

"What were you all talking about earlier?" Rip asked, after I picked which of the cattle dogs were going with me.

"They made me promise that if one of the wranglers ever makes me uncomfortable that I'll tell you about it," I explained.

"What brought that up?" Rip asked, as we started for the cabin. "Did someone do something?"

"Not recently enough to do anything." I explained the situation with Fred. I looked over to find Rip fuming silently. "I took care of it myself, at the time."

"That ever happens again, you let me handle it."

"Yes, sir."

"Fred won't be a problem ever again." I wasn't dumb enough to ask what that meant.

Rip walked me all the way back to my cabin, and made sure the dogs and I were inside before he left. I got changed, and let the dogs up on the bed after I was settled. I could hear my dad telling me that I was spoiling them, but I didn't care. They deserved a treat every now and then.

Once we were all situated, I turned off the light, and the dogs were snoring before I even got tired.

# Chapter 11

The next morning I had to be up and over to corrales because my dad was pricing stallions. I took the dogs back with me, and fed all of them before heading into the house to get a cup of coffee and a piece of toast.

"You're up early," Jamie commented, coming into the kitchen.

"I'm always up this early. You just never see me," I replied with an eye roll.

"Can we talk about what happened the other night?" he asked quietly.

"Depends on what you have to say," I said, finishing my toast.

"I just wanted to say that I'm sorry for what I said to you. That wasn't fair."

"No, it wasn't. I've never been anything but nice to you, and you turned on me like I was Beth. I don't know what the fuck happened to make you two hate each other that much, but I know I've never done anything to earn that treatment from you," I snapped.

"You're right. You might be the baby of the family, but you've always been the peacemaker," Jamie admitted. "I'm sorry."

"Thank you." I took a sip of my coffee before continuing. "Are either of you ever going to tell me what the hell makes you hate each other so much?"

Jamie shook his head. "You don't want to know."

"Just stop poking the bear," I told him as we went outside to go meet Travis, who was pulling up to the barn.

"Are you okay with this?" Jamie asked, keeping his voice low.

"Yeah," I shrugged. "I'm the one who ended it with him," I mumbled. "Besides, that was months ago." I broke things off with Travis just before I met Ryan. My friends told me I needed a night out without being attached to anyone, and then I met Ryan - and we all know how that ended.

"Morning Charlie!" Travis called, getting out of his truck.

"Hey, Travis," I smiled. When we were close enough, we hugged. "It's been a while."

"It has. Let me take you to dinner this week, and we can catch up," he offered.

"I don't know if that's a good idea."

"It'll be fun."

"I don't doubt that," I replied.

Mercifully, my father came down to the barn, and started asking Travis what he was bringing to show us this morning.

About an hour later, I was standing at the fence with my dad, Jamie, and Rip, watching the horses when I sensed motion behind me. I turned to find Monica and Tate standing there. I pulled away, and crossed to them.

"Hi Monica," I smiled. "What are you guys doing here?" Kayce wasn't at the ranch, so I really had no idea what would bring Monica.

Monica wasn't smiling. "Kayce was arrested."

"For what?" I asked.

"They wouldn't tell me anything," she replied.

"Who is "they"?"

"I'm not sure."

I gave her a sign to wait right there, while I turned to get my dad and Jamie. I stepped over to Jamie and told him what Monica said. He told our dad, and he whipped around to look at Tate and Monica. He walked over and reassured them everything would be okay.

I was standing at the fence when Travis' horse nudged my shoulder. I turned around to look at him, "Yes?" I smiled.

"Is everything okay?" Travis asked.

"When isn't something on fire in my family?" I replied, reaching up to pet the horse. "Did my dad pick anything yet?"

"Not yet." He changed topics on me, "I was serious about dinner."

"So was I."

"Are you seeing someone?" Travis asked.

"I am. I'm not really interested in messing that up," I replied.

"Did you break up with me because of this other guy?" Travis asked, getting down from the horse.

I shook my head, "No, I met him right after I broke up with you."

"Why did you break up with me?" Travis asked, leaning on the fence.

I didn't want to have this conversation, but it was bound to happen eventually. "I couldn't keep up with you."

"What the fuck does that mean?" he asked, just barely above a whisper.

"It means that you live such a different life than I do. I felt so out of place in your world," I explained. He's a horrible flirt, but that wasn't why I ended it. I couldn't take my place on the Yellowstone, and be with him at the same time.

He was silent for a few moments, and nodded. "You weren't out of place, Charlie. I'm sorry I didn't make you feel more at home."

"I'm not sure there was anything you could do. I've always been destined to end up right back here," I replied.

"Are you okay with me going to that dinner for your dad next week? We bought the tickets when we were still together," he asked.

"Yeah, of course."

"Good. I hope this new guy makes you happy. That's all I ever wanted."

"He does. You deserve someone better than me, who can keep up with you, and isn't tied down quite the way I am. We've been friends since high school, and I hope I can still call you my friend."

Travis nodded, "If there's ever anything I can do, all you have to do is ask."

"I appreciate that."

"I'll see you next week."

I stepped away to let Travis get finished packing up. It was clear that whatever was going on with Kayce has taken precedence. I made it up to the house just as the chopper was being called for.

"He's on the Reservation," Jamie told me. "I'm going to go get him."

"Thank you."

"Did you and Travis have a good talk?"  he asked.

I nodded. "Did I hear that you're running for Attorney General?" I asked, trying to deflect and change the subject. I'd overheard the conversation in the house over the last few days, but I hadn't remembered to ask.

Jamie chuckled, "Yes, I am. My campaign office opens next week."

"That's really cool. You've got my vote."

Before either of us could continue, the chopper landed on the lawn several yards away. It was time for Jamie to go get Kayce back.

"Bring him home, please." I'm not sure Jamie heard me.

I walked over to where Tate and Monica were sitting on the porch. "Jamie's good. If he can't bring him home, no one can," I told them. I'm not sure who I was lying to - them or myself.

"Thanks, Charlie."

"I've got to get to work. Will you call me when they get back?" I asked.

"Sure."

I walked back down to the barn to get my horse saddled so I could go meet the cowboys who had started doctoring the cows in pasture seven. They hadn't gotten very far by the time I got there. I got them to pick up the pace, and we were done by time Jamie and Kayce got back. I heard the chopper just as we were finishing the last one.

"Perfect timing!" I sighed.

"Go, we're pretty much done here," Lloyd replied.

"Thanks." I looked over at Ryan, "Can I talk to you later?" I asked quietly.

"Yeah. Is something wrong?" he asked.

"No. We just need to have the history talk," I mumbled. "I'd prefer it if you heard it from me, and not from one of my siblings."

"Okay. I'll come find you later."

"Thanks."

I rode back to the main house and tied my horse up. As I was getting off my horse, I saw Rip's truck pull down by the barn. He had someone new - at the very least, it wasn't someone I recognized at that distance.

"Grandpa said we can stay tonight!" Tate exclaimed just as I walked up to the group containing Kayce, Monica, my dad, and Tate.

"I don't know," Kayce started.

"We could all use a break," Monica cut in.

"It's settled. Tate can stay in the main house with me. You guys can take one of the cabins," my dad replied. "And Charlie will come up for dinner."

"I'll come up for dinner, but I'm sleeping in my cabin," I cut in.

"Fine."

...

I think that was probably the tamest family dinner in Dutton family history. It's easier when Beth isn't there. One way or another, she ends up storming out.

When we were done with dinner, I excused myself to go back to my cabin. "Don't forget the dogs!" my dad called.

"Dogs?" Kayce and Tate asked.

I stopped and turned back around, "Everyone is very concerned about me living on my own so far out into the ranch. The compromise was that I take a couple of the cattle dogs with me."

"You've got a gun, right?" Kayce asked.

"A pistol, a rifle, and a stun gun or two." I repeated, for what felt like the millionth time.

"Good."

"I'll see you in the morning," I yawned, hugging my twin brother.

I was closing up the barn after getting the same two dogs from the night before, when Ryan found me. "Hi," I yawned.

"Are you okay?" he asked, as we headed for my cabin.

"Yeah. It's just been a long day. Um, you saw the horses in the arena this morning?" I asked.

"They were a little hard to miss."

"I dated the guy that set all of that up for about two years before we got together," I admitted, looking over at Ryan.

He was silent for a few minutes."Why are you just telling me now?"

"We've been doing this for about six months. I wanted to be honest with you. I'd also rather have you hear it from me, than one of my siblings when they're out for revenge for god knows what. Not to mention he's going to be at the Livestock Association dinner for my dad next week."

Ryan looked like he was trying to choose his words carefully. "Who ended it?"

"I did."

"Why?"

"Because it's hard to have a relationship with someone constantly on the road, when you're tied down to one place," I replied. "I always felt like an inconvenience when I did take time to go with him. I used to show horses like that before I had to go to vet school. It was always a reminder that I gave up something I loved to serve the ranch."

"Are you saying that you settled for me?" Ryan stopped walking.

I stopped short, and turned to look at him. "That's not what I mean," I said, trying not to cry. "I wouldn't trade this for anything. I know what I want, and it's not him. I do believe in serendipity, and things happening for a reason. Some force bigger than you and me put me back here for a reason. It put us here, together, for a reason."

Ryan shook his head, "I won't be some consolation prize because you had to give up the life you "loved"."

I was getting frustrated, trying to keep from saying something that I'd regret later. I just felt defeated. "I love you. I just wanted to be honest with you. You deserve that. If you're done with me, I understand." I turned and started to walk away, the dogs at my heels.

"Wait, Charlie!" Ryan called, walking to catch up. "I'm not done with you. I don't think I will ever be done with you." I let him put his hands on my hips, and pull me closer. "I'm just trying to process."

I put my arms around his neck and leaned in to kiss him. "You have absolutely nothing to worry about. In the two years that I was with Travis, he only ever told me he loved me twice, and once was after I broke up with him."

"I won't make that mistake." Ryan kissed me again. "I love you."

"I love you too."

# Chapter 12

It didn't take much to convince Ryan to come back to the cabin to take a shower with me. We were in there until the water got cold...

"There's no chance you can stay, is there?" I asked, handing him a towel.

"Not tonight," he replied, drying his hair off. "I swear, one of these times, I will figure out a way to be able to spend the night with you."

"I'll hold you to that." I said, putting my shirt on. Once he was dressed again, I pulled him in for one more kiss before he left.

As Ryan was headed out the door, he nearly collided with Kayce. "Shit," Ryan mumbled.

Kayce just shook his head and stepped aside so Ryan could go. Once Ryan was gone, Kayce came inside, shut the door, and busted up laughing. "You should have seen the look on his face!"

"I imagine it looked something like it did when Rip caught us," I replied.

He laughed for another minute or so. "God, I needed that." He took off his boots and hat.

I yawned, and motioned for him to follow me back to my room. "Not that I'm not happy to see you, but I figured you and Monica would be taking full advantage of the child-free privacy." I sat down, leaning back against the headboard. I let the dogs up on the bed after I was comfortable. "What brings you to my neck of the woods?"

Kayce was about to sit down, "Did you guys...?"

"In the shower. So unless you're planning on sleeping in my tub, you can sit down." I teased.

He sat down on the other end of the bed, moving one of the border collies out of his way. "Monica said she wanted to use the time here to forget about stuff at home, and the next thing I know, she wants to talk about giving Tate this life." He shifted back to a more serious tone.

"So you got up and came over here?" I asked, just to clarify.

"I left this place for a reason. I had to get out from under his shadow. He wanted Monica to get an abortion, and now he wants to play grandfather," Kayce vented.

I stayed silent. I'll never forget that night... The night that our father branded Kayce, it took two ranch hands to keep me down.

"This is how you prove you can be trusted," our father said, pointing the brand at Kayce.

"What the fuck?" Kayce and I replied in unison.

I stumbled upon the scene on accident. Clearly, I wasn't meant to see this. Dad tried to get me to leave, but I wouldn't budge. When I wouldn't leave, he went ahead with it anyway.

"You're insane," I shook my head. "What would Mom think?" I asked. "I have a hard time believing she'd let you do this."

He pointed the hot brand in my face, "Keep talking and you'll be next."

"I'm not the one who will have to live with the consequences of that," I replied.

"Hold him down," my father said, nodding to Rip and Lloyd. "Make sure she doesn't interfere." He nodded in my direction.

In a split second, I watched Rip and Lloyd fight and wrestle Kayce to the ground, as I tried to fight off, and get around the other two ranch hands. I scratched and clawed at them to try to get to Kayce, but it was no use. My father already had the brand on Kayce's chest as Rip and Lloyd held him down. The noises coming from Kayce still haunt my nightmares to this day.

When he was done, they let Kayce up, but the other hands still had me restrained. One of them forced me to my knees in front of my father.

"You touch her, and I will kill you," Kayce said, stepping in front of me.

"I think you missed the point of what that brand means," our father replied.

"I won't let you hurt her. You made your point. Put the iron down," Kayce said.

There was a long pause before my father dropped iron on the ground. "Let her go."

Kayce turned around and helped me up off the ground...

"I don't know how you came back after that night," Kayce said, shaking his head.

"To be honest, I don't know either. I didn't know what else to do." That wasn't entirely true, and I hated keeping secrets from Kayce.

"You could have been a champion. Hell, I bet you still could."

"I like my job. I wish I worked for someone else, but I like taking care of the animals," I replied. "I try to stay out of the lodge as much as possible."

"You have a skill set that you could take to any ranch."

"I know."

"So why don't you?"

"Everyone I love is here." I said quietly. "What I do know is that the only way problems in a marriage get worked out is if you talk to your spouse. It's a conversation worth having, if anything, just to make her understand."

Kayce grumbled and rubbed his face. "Why do you always have to be right?"

"It's my superpower," I giggled. "You know what I did tonight? I had to tell Ryan about Travis. For a minute, I thought he was going to break up with me."

"How did you go from that to shower sex?" Kayce laughed.

"Honest communication. You should give it a try."

"Fine, you win."

"You're welcome to crash here tonight. The couch is comfortable, and I've washed the bedding in Lee's room, if you're comfortable with that?" I told him.

"No, I should go back to Monica," Kayce replied, getting up off the bed.

"Good call."

"'Night, Charlie."

"Goodnight, Kayce."

Part of the reason I came home was because my Dad told me he had cancer. He needed someone to help him, but he made me promise not to tell anyone - including Jamie and Lee, who were living on the ranch at the time. I was the diversion.

I kept my promise.

...

The next day was eventful, to say the least. I was with Kayce when he got the call about Monica. She was injured trying to break up a fight. I went with him and my dad to the school.

My father grouched the whole way back to the ranch. "Kayce's never going to learn what he needs to, to run this place." He changed topics after receiving a phone call from the Governor, relaying what happened when she met with Beth and Jamie.

"If you're waiting for me to feign shock that Beth disrespected Montana's highest ranking government official, it's not going to happen," I replied when he repeated what was said.

"Jesus. Maybe I should have sent you instead."

"I'm better with animals."

The ride back to the ranch was quiet for the most part. I'm not sure how Beth and Jamie managed to beat us back, but they did. "This is new," I mumbled, seeing Beth and Jamie standing together, waiting for us to get back.

Dad put the window down when he stopped, "What?"

"Talk to us about cancer," Jamie said.

I felt my stomach drop.

"How long have you had it?" Beth asked.

My father put up a finger, put the window back up and turned on me. "You had one job!" He snapped. "Say nothing! You couldn't even do that right."

I shook my head frantically, "I didn't say anything!"

There was a sharp rap on the window. "Why did she get to know?" Jamie asked through the window.

"I didn't say a fucking word. So don't blame me for this shit!" I snapped and got out of the truck, slamming the door.

"Easy," My dad growled, getting out.

"Tell that to the person shooting holes into the roof of that truck," I said, pointing to Jamie's truck.

It didn't take much to put two and two together on who told them about Dad's cancer. "So, who told the Governor about the cancer?" I asked, looking over at Jamie.

"I'm not touching that until you tell me why you kept this shit to yourself," Jamie replied.

"I told her not to say anything," Dad cut in. "One of my kids can apparently do as they're told. Who was it?"

"Your doctor talks too much. His father is the head of the cattlemen's association," Jamie explained. "Does Kayce know?"

"No." I shook my head.

My father turned his anger on Beth next. "Come with me. We're going to have a conversation about your behavior." He led her into the house, and I took that as my cue to bolt.

Jamie followed me as I turned to walk down to the barn. "Why the fuck did you keep that to yourself?"

I didn't stop, or turn to face him. "I know you keep much worse secrets for him than the one I kept," I replied.

"I'm not keeping them from my family!" Jamie shouted.

"No, the only secret you keep from your family is why Beth hates you so much!" I snapped, rounding on him. He's already taller than me, but he was further up the hill than I was, so he towered over me.

"Charlie!" I heard someone call my name in the distance.

"What?!" I yelled, spinning to see who was talking to me. It was Rip. He waved me over. I left Jamie standing where he was, but I flipped the bird in his direction as I left.

Rip wasn't alone. He was standing with a new cowboy I'd never met. "Everything okay?" Rip asked, once I was close enough that we could talk at normal volumes.

"Probably safe to assume the answer is no when I'm screaming at someone. I like to think I don't do that very often," I replied.

"If you have a minute, we could use your help," he said. I knew he was trying to redirect me, and keep me from making a scene with Jamie for all to see.

"Sure."

"I'm Walker," the cowboy said, extending his hand.

"Charlie," I replied, shaking his hand.

Rip walked us back to the barn. On the way down, he made the comment that he had seen a bear on the ranch that morning. "We'll need to haze it off the property if it sticks around."

"Please tell me that's not what you called me down here to do," I moaned.

Rip took his sunglasses off, and I noticed bruising around his eyes. I'd noticed similar bruises on Kayce this morning, but kept my mouth shut. I guess there's still some tension there...

"No. Truthfully, I just needed to separate you and Jamie," Rip replied. He dismissed Walker and told him to wait in the bunkhouse.

I was seething, and just wanted to be alone before I said something I regretted. "I'm done for today. I've had my integrity questioned, and I've been pushed to my limit. I'm going home. Anyone who comes near my cabin, it's at their own peril." I stomped out of the barn, and headed for my cabin.

(I'm publishing this on my phone, so I apologize if there are formatting issues.)

# Chapter 13

When I got home, I locked the door behind me, not wanting to be disturbed. I stripped and took a bath, trying to relax.

A couple hours later, I was dozing off on the couch when there was a knock on my door. I ignored it at first, but they tapped again. "Fuck off!" I called.

"It's Ryan," he called back. "I have dinner, and the dogs."

I grudgingly got up off the couch and looked out the window to make sure he was alone before letting him inside.

"Rip said I probably had the best chance at not getting murdered," Ryan said, stepping inside. The dogs ran inside, jumping up on the couch.

"Yeah, sorry about that. I figured you were my dad or Jamie. It's not been a great day."

"Do you want to talk about it?" he asked, putting a bowl of soup down on my kitchen counter.

"Probably best to just let it go."

Ryan sat down at the table, "I was told that I had to stay until you eat that." He pointed to the bowl on the counter.

"And if I don't decide to eat it until breakfast?" I replied.

Ryan chuckled, sensing where I was going with this. "You need to eat something. I know you didn't come in for lunch today."

"But I didn't really work that much today," I replied. "Did Rip actually say that you had to stay until I ate that, or did he just say you had to stay until I ate something?"

"He specified that bowl of soup," Ryan said.

"How about this, I'll eat something else tonight, and have that for breakfast in the morning? That way, you can spend the night, and still be following orders?" I asked.

"That's a compromise I can live with," he chuckled.

"So take your boots off and get comfortable." I smiled and put the soup in the fridge and grabbed the leftover hamburger helper. "Have you had dinner?"

"Yeah, I ate before I came over."

"Do you want any of this?" I asked, gesturing to the casserole dish.

"Maybe a little bit."

I chuckled to myself and made a couple plates. Once everything was warm, I brought both plates back to the table with forks. We ate dinner pretty quickly before we moved over to the couch.

I made the dogs move so we could sit down. Well, I sat down. Ryan stretched out and put his head in my lap. It dawned on me that he was wearing different clothes than I'd seen him in this morning. He had on sweatpants and a t-shirt. I'd only ever seen him in sweatpants when he was done for the day. I ran my fingers through his hair to find it was already clean. He showered before he ever came over here. Ryan spending the night was the plan all along.

"So whose idea was this?" I asked, looking down at Ryan.

"I don't know what you're talking about," he smiled up at me.

"Bullshit," I laughed.

"It was a joint effort. He did tell me to stay until you ate that. I told him he had to know how you'd exploit it, and he was fine with it," Ryan replied.

"I knew he was a big softie under all of that macho bullshit!"

"He asked that we keep that to ourselves for now," he said.

"Deal. That's a secret I'll happily keep."

"Is that what happened with Jamie? He was keeping secrets?" Ryan asked. "I saw what happened this afternoon, but I couldn't hear."

I ran my fingers through his hair. "I was the one keeping secrets. I was told to keep a secret, and it got out without me saying a word. It wasn't my fault."

To his credit, Ryan didn't ask me what the secret was. "I know it wasn't." He sat up and kissed me, wrapping me in his arms. When we parted, I laid my head against his shoulder. This is what I'd been needing.

"Thank you," I yawned.

"What for?"

"For staying."

"I told you I'd find a way." He scooped me up in his arms and carried me back to my room and dropped me unceremoniously on my bed, causing me to laugh.

I'd already been in my pjs, so I got under the covers. Ryan quickly took off his pants before diving under the covers with me. "I could get used to this," he smiled, leaning over to kiss me.

"I could too." I rested my head against his chest and he wrapped an arm around me. I found myself absentmindedly tracing patterns on his side as we laid there in a comfortable silence.

Just as I was drifting off to sleep both of the dogs jumped up on the bed, scaring both of us. We laughed, and rearranged so that we all fit on the bed together. I had my back to Ryan's chest, and he pulled me close. I had one of the dogs by my knees, and the other was tucked into Ryan's.

"You spoil them," Ryan teased through a yawn.

"So?" I asked. "I never got to have a house dog growing up. I love getting to have two now." I smiled. "Not that I'll admit that to anyone else."

Ryan chuckled, "I promise I won't tell."

"Good. If you do, I'll deny it until I'm blue in the face."

"I'll keep your secret." I felt him smile as he kissed the back of my neck.

"I love you," I mumbled.

"Me too."

I slept better that night than I had in a while. Neither of us were ready when my alarm went off in the morning. "Make it stop," he groaned, and I fumbled for the off switch.

"I don't want to move," I moaned, pulling the blankets up to my chin.

"You and I both know that Rip will be at that door if we aren't out of here forty-five minutes," he said, sitting up.

"You're not wrong." I sat up. Neither of the dogs budged. "They usually don't move until I open the front door."

We got up and got dressed before moving out to the kitchen. I grabbed the bowl of soup out of the fridge while Ryan started the coffee pot.

"I have that thing for my dad tonight. I need to be done early," I mentioned, warming up the bowl in the microwave.

"What thing?"

"The dinner. I was told a dress was mandatory, no boots."

Ryan chuckled. "So what you're telling me is that I need to find my way up by the lodge when it's time for you to leave?"

"I'm not telling you anything," I teased.

We ate breakfast and just before he left, I pulled him in close by the shirt, and kissed him hard. "We need to find a way to do this again."

"We will." He kissed me again before leaving for the bunkhouse.

...

I ran into Rip while I was out for a ride later that morning. He rode over and we rode together for a bit. "Thank you," I said after a few moments of silence.

"What for?" he asked.

"You know what. I needed last night."

"He told you what my condition was, right? Rip asked.

"That I tell no one that you were involved? Yes, he told me, and I won't say anything," I replied.

"Good, but I'm glad to know you're feeling better this morning."

"I am."

"You need to be careful out here. I'm serious when I say there's a bear out here. I've seen it, and so has Kayce," he explained.

"I believe you."

"I'll probably have the boys deal with it this afternoon or tomorrow," he told me.

I nodded and we rode for a while in silence before I peeled off to go check on the cattle out in the pasture.

I finished everything on my list for that day around 2:30 in the afternoon. After unsaddling my horse, and putting her back in the barn, I made the trek back to the cabin to shower and get ready. I curled my hair into long waves and applied light makeup before grabbing my dress, shoes, and tights to head up to the house.

"Hot date tonight?" Colby called, as I passed him and Lloyd in the field.

"Not really. Big formal dinner for my Dad," I yelled back. I could hear them laughing as I walked off.

"I thought you were going to be ready by the time you got here?" My dad snapped as I walked into the house.

"Yeah, I'm going to go for a walk through the field, in a dress and heels," I responded with an eye roll. "All I have to do is get dressed."

I walked up to my room and changed into a full length, strapless, maroon dress with black, sheer tights, and black stilettos. I threw my phone into my clutch before I did one last mirror check before going back downstairs. "Happy? Took less than ten minutes," I said, meeting my Dad in the kitchen.

"You look nice," he replied.

"Thank you. Is anyone else joining us?" I asked.

"I have no idea." I took that as a "no".

We had to make a stop on the way to dinner because we saw a bus load of tourists standing in our field, all staring at a grizzly bear that was only a few feet away. I made a mental note to tell Rip that I'd seen the bear.

"They're going to get eaten," I mumbled.

"They're trespassing," my dad snapped. He pulled the truck off to the side of the road and put it in park. "Stay." He said, retrieving the rifle from the backseat.

"No arguments here." I'm not wearing the right shoes for this. I watched him talk to who I presumed was the tour guide to try to get them to leave. When that didn't work, he fired the rifle in the air twice. That got them to move a bit faster. Once they were gone, he got back in the truck, and we left.

When we finally got to the event center, we were shown to our table. My dad got up to mingle before dinner started, and I stayed seated. I hated my shoes, and wanted to be off my feet for as long as possible.

"Wow, you look incredible," Travis said, coming to stand next to my chair. He was wearing a three piece suit and matching hat.

"You clean up pretty well yourself," I smiled. "Are you going to stand all night, or have a seat?" I asked, gesturing for him to have a seat. His name card was next to mine. There were places saved for Beth and Jamie on my dad's other side. A few other people that I didn't know had also joined the table.

I felt my phone buzz against the table as Travis sat down. "Have you thought about getting back out on the circuit again?" he asked. "I've got a couple good horses that I could use a rider for."

I shrugged. "It's hard right now, but you're not the first person to suggest that to me in the last week," I replied. My phone buzzed again.

"Someone else trying to scoop you up?" Travis asked.

"No, Kayce suggested it."

My father came back to the table and gave us a skeptical look. He didn't have an opportunity to say anything because he was being called up to the podium to give a few remarks and the blessing before dinner was served.

My phone buzzed a couple times during the blessing. "Maybe you should check that?" Travis asked as my dad was making his way back to the table.

"Someone clearly wants my attention." I pulled my phone out and saw several long text messages from Kayce. Monica was in the hospital, and it was serious. She'd been hit in the head the day before, and required brain surgery. "Sorry, I'll be right back." I got up from the table and went into the hallway to call my brother.

"She's back in surgery right now," Kayce told me. "Tate and I are just in the waiting room. They really didn't say how long it would be."

"Do you want me to come wait with you?" I asked.

"Can I ask you to come get Tate and watch him for tonight? I don't want him to see Monica until we know she's going to be okay."

"That's not a problem. Dad and I can be there when this dinner is over," I told Kayce.

"Thanks Charlie."

"You don't have to thank me for anything. Family is supposed to support each other. I'll text you when we're headed your way. I have to get back in there."

"What was that?" my dad asked when I sat back down.

I filled him and Travis in on what I learned from Kayce, and that we needed to pick Tate up from the hospital on the way home.

He swore under his breath, "Is she going to be okay?"

"It's too early to know." I felt sick to my stomach with worry.

"Is there anything I can do?" Travis asked.

"Not really. It's just a waiting game now."

"If you don't want to wait, I can take you to the hospital to get Tate, and take you back to the ranch?" he offered. I think he could sense my nerves.

"You don't have to do that," I replied quietly.

"I want to. I know this is the last place you'd rather be, knowing someone you care about is in the hospital," Travis said.

"Go ahead, Charlotte. I'll catch up with you at home." My dad nodded, and the look on his face told me we'd be talking about this later.

"Okay." I nodded and got up from the table, following Travis out to the parking lot. He helped me up into his truck before getting into the driver's side. I texted Kayce to let him know as we pulled out of the parking lot.

"Are you going to be okay?" Travis asked.

"Yeah. I'm just really worried about her." I needed her to be okay more for Kayce's sake than anything. I worried what he would do if she didn't make it. "And exhausted from the usual family bullshit."

"Sounds like you need some time off," he said.

I chuckled a little bit. "Time off doesn't really exist in my world these days. The most I can hope for is a few stolen minutes of peace and quiet."

"Time off exists in my world."

"I call bullshit on that one. I don't think you took any time off in the two years we were together," I replied.

"I said it exists. I didn't say I used it."

"As long as we're both being honest with ourselves."

Travis walked me into the hospital, and we were getting plenty of looks. Kayce stood up, and pulled me aside. "What's he doing here?" he asked quietly.

"He was nice enough to give me a ride from the Livestock Association dinner so I didn't have to wait for Dad."

"Why was he at the dinner?"

"I'm not doing this with you right now. You're not going to have a go at me while your wife is down the hall, fighting for her life," I snapped in a hushed tone.

I watched him visibly relax. "You're right. Thank you for taking Tate for the night."

"You're welcome."

Kayce called Tate over and told him that he was going to go stay with me for a night or two, which he seemed okay with as long as he got updates on his mom's condition.

I hugged Kayce before we left for the ranch. I knew even though we were going home, my night wasn't over by a long shot.

# Chapter 14

Travis dropped us off up at the lodge. On the way home, I texted Rip to ask him to meet us at the lodge with a couple ATVs so that we don't have to walk all the way back to my cabin.

When we got there, Rip and Ryan were waiting for us. Travis helped me down out of his truck before leaving us. "Let me run up and get changed before we head back," I told them. I left Tate outside with them.

I went inside, taking my shoes off as soon as I was in the door. I headed upstairs, and quickly changed back into the clothes I was wearing earlier before heading back outside.

"Tate, you ride with me," Rip said, getting Tate's attention.

"Okay."

I climbed up behind Ryan, and he turned to whisper, "Are you okay?"

"Better than Monica is doing," I mumbled.

"I'm not going to pick a fight about Travis, for what it's worth. I trust you," he told me as he started the ATV.

"I love you," I sighed, wrapping my arms around him. I felt my body release the tension it was holding, as I melted against him.

"Let's go," Rip called.

We took off for the cabin, and there was no talking. I didn't have the energy to yell over the engine. When we got there, the dogs were sitting on the porch, waiting patiently.

"They ran over after I fed them tonight," Rip said.

"That's funny. Clearly, we have a routine now," I replied.

"Are you guys hungry?" Ryan asked.

I was going to say no, but my stomach growled and answered for me. "I'm hungry too," Tate replied.

"Gator left a couple extra steaks in the bunkhouse. I'll run them back over," Ryan told us.

"That's a great idea," Rip nodded.

"Hey Tate, will you take the dogs in? You can make yourself at home and turn on the tv. I need a minute," I told him.

"Sweet!" He was off like a shot into the cabin, closing the door behind him.

"Do you need me for this minute?" Rip asked, once the three of us were alone.

"Nope. Thank you for helping us get out here. It's one thing if it's just me. It's harder with someone who doesn't know the terrain," I replied.

"Will Monica be okay?"

"We don't know yet. Kayce is going to call me in the morning when he knows more," I replied.

"Just let me know if I can help. I'll give you a minute alone." Rip nodded, and took off on his ATV again.

Ryan climbed off the ATV, "Come here." He pulled me into a hug and held me tight while I shook, trying not to cry. "I'm serious. I love you, and I trust you. I don't care about him. I'm not thrilled that he gave you a ride, but there are bigger things to worry about right now."

"I love you too. I'm so scared for her. It scares me to think about what will happen to Kayce if she doesn't make it," I said quietly.

"Don't borrow that trouble yet," Ryan replied. He kissed my forehead and stepped back. "I'm going to go grab those steaks, and I'll be right back."

"Thank you," I sniffed. I wiped my eyes, hoping that it didn't look like I'd been crying. "I'll keep an ear out for you."

When Ryan was gone, I went inside. Turns out Tate and the dogs were very comfortable. They were lying in a pile on the couch. "I think they like you," I chuckled, coming around in front of the couch.

"I wish I had a dog," Tate replied. "This is awesome."

Ryan was gone maybe fifteen minutes before he came back with a small cooler. "Thank you."

"I love you, Charlie. Please promise me you'll eat. I know you don't when you get anxious," Ryan said.

"I will. It'll help with how shaky I feel," I replied quietly.

Ryan kissed my temple, and got back on the ATV.

As he left, I went back inside to fix dinner for Tate and I. I opened the cooler to find containers of mashed potatoes and gravy packed in with the steaks. I plated everything and warmed it up before asking Tate to come eat at the table.

"Why can't I eat over here?" he protested.

"Because Things 1 and 2 will clean the plate before you get a bite," I replied.

"That's fair," he said, extricating himself from the dog pile.

We ate dinner in silence, both feeling the exhaustion of the day. When we were done, I put the plates in the sink to deal with later.

While we were eating, I agonized over where to have him sleep. On the one hand, he could sleep in Lee's room, but that just made my stomach turn in knots. The more I thought about it, I didn't think I was ready for someone else to sleep in there just yet. If someone was going to sleep in there, I'd rather it be me.

"You'll sleep in here," I told Tate, showing him to my room. I grabbed my clothes out from under one of the pillows. "The dogs will probably sleep on the bed with you, for what it's worth. If you don't like that, we can close the door, and I'll make them sleep in the other room with me."

"They can stay. I want them to sleep on me."

"Don't tell anyone they slept on the bed. Technically, I'm not supposed to spoil them, but I don't see the problem with them sleeping on the bed," I smiled.

"Deal."

"Get some sleep. We'll call your dad first thing in the morning," I told him.

"Night, Charlie."

"Goodnight Tate."

I left him to his own devices, and went to turn off the lights before I went to bed myself when there was a light tap on the door. I groaned internally and put my clothes down on the couch before answering the door.

"Dad? What are you doing out here so late?" I asked, stepping outside, and closing the door behind me.

"I just wanted to make sure everything was okay," he replied, gesturing to the chairs on the porch.

"It's as okay as it's going to be right now. Tate's in my room, and I'm staying in Lee's," I explained, taking a seat. "We'll call Kayce in the morning for an update."

"That's good." He sat down next to me. "Are you and Travis seeing each other?"

"That's quite the transition," I mumbled.

"You didn't answer me."

"We aren't seeing each other anymore. We were at the time we made those reservations. He asked if he could still go when he came up this week," I explained.

"Who ended it?" my father asked.

"I'm really not in the mood to do this," I replied. "It doesn't matter who ended it because we're still friends. It didn't end badly by any stretch of the imagination. He wouldn't keep asking me if I wanted back out on the circuit again if he hated my guts."

"Do you want to go back to cutting and reining?"

"I don't know." Admittedly, the offer was tempting, but I'm too invested with Ryan right now to really consider it. I don't want to be away that long.

"I don't like that you thought you had to keep it a secret that you were seeing him," my father commented.

"It wasn't a secret. Everyone knew."

"Does everyone know about you and Ryan?"

I think I dislocated something in my neck, turning to face him so quickly. "How?"

He chuckled, "There's nothing that happens on this ranch that I don't know about." There's a long pause. "Does he make you happy, Charlotte?"

I nodded, "He does. I love him."

"I don't love the idea of you seeing one of the Wranglers, but of the bunch, he's probably the best choice," he shrugged. "I expect you to keep it professional when you're both on duty. Is that understood?"

"Yes, sir." I could feel just how hot my face was. It had to be bright red to match. "Can we keep the fact that you know about this between us for now? I'll let him in on the secret, but does everyone else need to know?"

"I won't say anything."

"Thank you."

He stood up, and pulled me up and into a hug. "I hope you know that you can always come to me. You don't need to keep secrets, and I'll support your decision to leave the ranch, if that's what you decide."

"You're stuck with me for a while." Everyone I loved was here, and there was no way I would leave Kayce right now.

"Glad to hear it. Why don't you go inside, and get some sleep?"

"Yep. I'm exhausted."

We hugged again before he started off for the lodge, and I went back inside. The light in Tate's room was turned off. I grabbed my clothes and went into Lee's room. I changed quickly, and looked down at the bed. "It's just me. I hope this is okay," I muttered. "I'm sorry."

I turned the light off and got in bed, pulling the blanket up to my nose. Even though I'd washed it, it still smelled faintly like my brother's cologne. I took a couple long deep breaths and closed my eyes.

I fell asleep relatively quickly that night, and started dreaming almost instantly.

I kept hearing my name being called in the distance. "Charlie, I need to know you can hear me," the voice said gently.

"Five more minutes," I begged, burrowing deeper under the blankets. I felt the bed sag as someone sat down. They put a hand on my shoulder and shook gently.

"Charlie."

I looked up to see Lee sitting over me. "What are you doing here?" I asked, trying to wake myself up.

"You're the one sleeping in my bed, genius," he chuckled.

"Sorry," I mumbled, attempting to get up.

He pushed me back down. "Stay. I understand why you chose to sleep in here. I promise my intent was not to just give you crap about sleeping in here."

"Please say you're not a ghost who's stuck here," I replied.

Lee shook his head. "I'm not stuck anywhere, Charlie. I'm okay. I just came back because there's something you need to know."

"What?"

"It's okay to leave if you want to. You're not stuck here either," he said.

"The land or the ranch?"

"Both."

"The only reason I don't leave is because everyone I care about is here. Otherwise, Travis' offer is really tempting."

"Well, I'm proud of you, no matter what you decide. I know you know this, but I'm going to say it anyway. You deserve to be happy. Build a life for yourself that makes you happy. You don't have to live for Dad. Be more than what he turned each of us into." Lee's grip on my shoulder got tighter as he spoke. "I have to go Charlie. Love you little sister."

"I miss you every day."

I woke up with a start, looking around the room to find that I was alone. I looked at the clock on the nightstand: 1:04am. I took a deep breath, and resituated to get comfortable. "I hear you," I mumbled. "I hear you."

# Chapter 15

The next morning I slept in a bit because of our late night. What got me up was the dogs' whining. "I hear you," I mumbled as I got up to let them out. It was just after 7am. Tate came stumbling out of my room, rubbing his eyes.

"How did you sleep?" I asked.

"Fine. Can we call my dad?" he replied.

"He may not have had a chance to see the doctor this morning yet, but we can check in with him," I said, going back into Lee's room to get my phone.

I called Kayce as I walked back out into the living room. I put it on speaker as I sat down on the couch. My brother picked up on the third or fourth ring. "Hey Kayce, you're on speaker. It's just me and Tate."

"Hey Buddy, did you have a good night?" he asked.

"I got to sleep with two dogs," Tate grinned.

"Narc," I laughed.

"Your secret is safe with me," Kayce chuckled.

"How's Monica doing?" I asked. I was afraid he was trying to put off telling Tate bad news.

Kayce let out a long sigh, "She made it through the surgery, but she's not out of the woods yet. They gave her medicine to make sure she slept through the night. She should be awake in a couple hours."

"Can I come see her today?" Tate asked.

There was a long pause.

"Yeah, I think so. Can you bring him by around lunchtime, Charlie?"

"Yeah, no problem," I nodded.

"Thanks. I'll let you know if the plan needs to change."

After we hung up, I took a quick shower and got ready for the day. I took Tate up to the main house for breakfast. I knew Gator would fix him just about anything he wanted.

Jamie came down as we were sitting at the breakfast bar. "Long time, no see," I smiled.

"Sorry. My campaign office opens today. I've been trying to get that up and running," he explained.

"Is that why you didn't go to dad's thing last night?" I asked.

He rolled his eyes, "Yes. Dad asked the same thing last night."

"Sorry."

"Did you go?" he asked.

"Technically I was there for about an hour. Kayce called, and Travis gave me a ride to go pick up Tate, and drove us back here."

Jamie looked visibly confused.

"My mom is in the hospital," Tate replied sadly.

"I'll fill you in later," I said, watching his eyes get wide. I followed him out of the kitchen into the hall. "I know you're really busy, but can you make some time for me later this afternoon? Can I drop by your office after I run him into town?"

"Yeah, I'll make it work. Are you okay?" Jamie asked.

"Yeah. It was an interesting night," I mumbled.

"I'll send you the address and tell Christina to send you back when you get there." With that, he left the house in a rush.

I walked back into the kitchen, "What do you want to do this morning?" I asked Tate, who was eating a plate of pancakes that was bigger than his head.

"Could we go for a ride?" Tate asked.

"I'd rather you didn't," my dad replied, joining us in the kitchen. "I've got the boys out looking for that bear this morning. Stay close to the house until they haze it out of here."

"There's a bear out there?" Tate asked.

"It's huge," I replied.

"Have you eaten Charlotte?" Dad cut in.

"I ate last night," I said. All I'd had this morning was a cup of coffee.

"Eat something this morning," he replied.

I turned to look at Gator, "Fruit or toast?" he asked.

"You know me so well. Toast is fine."

We finished our food pretty quickly, and headed down to the barn to see what we could do to help while the boys were out dealing with the bear.

...

After I dropped Tate off at the hospital, I drove over to Jamie's campaign office. When I walked in, no one noticed me at first, so I stood there, feeling a bit awkward. A woman with auburn hair walked over, "Are you a volunteer?" she asked.

"No. I'm here to see my brother," I replied. She looked confused. "Jamie."

"Oh! You're Charlotte! I'm Christina," she explained, extending her hand.

"I prefer Charlie," I said, shaking her hand.

She nodded. "Come on back. I know he's expecting you." Christina showed me back to Jamie's office.

When we got there she stepped in and closed the door behind the three of us. "I need to speak to him alone." I told her.

"Oh sorry, I'll just be outside," she said, leaving the office.

I closed the door behind her, and locked it. "I don't like her."

"You just met her," Jamie replied.

"She didn't do herself any favors calling me Charlotte, and she's nosy." I rolled my eyes, and sat down in the chair in front of the desk. "But she's not what I'm here to talk to you about."

"I'm really hoping you're going to tell me how Travis drove you home from Dad's thing last night," he said.

"That's probably the tamest bit of this story. We made the reservation when we were still together. He was there as my friend. Kayce called from the hospital and asked me to get Tate." I explained Monica's injuries.

"Are they going to press charges?" Jamie asked.

"I don't know."

"Is she going to be okay?"

"We don't know the full extent of the damage yet. Travis was kind enough to offer to take me to get Tate and bring us back home so that we didn't have to wait until dinner was over," I said.

"How did Ryan take it?" There was almost a smirk on his face.

"Like an adult," I snapped. I intentionally left out my conversation with our father after that comment. "I slept in Lee's room last night. It didn't seem right to have Tate stay in there."

"Are you okay? That must have been hard," he asked, softening up.

"Um, I had a dream where he woke me up to tell me to leave the ranch if I want, and to build a life that makes me happy. Not a life that makes Dad happy." I sniffed, trying to hold back tears.

"Come here," Jamie got up and stepped around the desk and pulled me up and into a hug as I started to cry. "He's right, though. Do what makes you happy."

"I know," I nodded, hugging my brother back.

"It's going to be okay."

Thankfully my face was buried in his shoulder, so he couldn't see me roll my eyes. I hate it when he says that. I pulled away, and wiped my eyes. "Sorry for bugging you. I needed to get that off my chest, and Kayce's not really the person to talk about that with..."

"You're not bugging me, Charlie. You can come by whenever you want. I'll make sure Christina backs off a bit."

"Thanks. I'll let you get back to it."

...

On my way home, I saw a saddled horse out in one of the fields without a rider in sight. I was on the ranch, so I pulled my car off to the side of the road, and got out, grabbing my rope out of the back seat.

Upon closer inspection, it was Jimmy's horse. "Why am I not surprised?"

"What happened, buddy?" I asked gently as I walked closer to the horse. "Why are you out here all by yourself?" I held out my hand and kept talking to the horse. "Let me help you. I can take you home, and we get all this stuff off of you."

I didn't even need the rope because the horse came to me with a little bit of coaxing. I grabbed the reins and got up into the saddle. Once I was situated, I rode back to the barn.

When I made it back, there was no one in sight. I jumped down and opened one of the pens, leading the horse inside. After shutting the gate, I set to work on taking all of the tack off of him, draping it all over the fence. "That's gotta feel better," I mumbled.

"Why is your car out in the middle of nowhere?" Rip asked, riding up to the pen.

"Because I had to bring this guy back in," I replied. "He was out in a field by himself. I'm guessing something happened, he spooked, and bucked Jimmy off."

"Dumbass," Rip replied, shaking his head. "Come on, I'll give you a ride back to your car, and you can put this stuff away when you get back."

"Sounds good." I hopped the fence and walked over to Rip's horse. He gave me a hand up, and we rode off toward my car.

"They were supposed to deal with the bear," Rip told me. "I sent Jimmy, Ryan, and Walker to either shoot it or haze it out of here earlier this morning."

"Judging by the fact that Jimmy got bucked, I'd say they found it."

"It's 50/50," Rip chuckled.

"I'll check the bunkhouse when I get back to see if they made it back."

After about twenty minutes we found my car. Rip stopped just in front, and helped me down. "Let me know if there's anything I can do to help," I smiled, getting back in the car.

"Will do."

I got in my car and made it back to the main house in about ten minutes. I walked back down to the barn to finish dealing with Jimmy's horse.

...

Once I finished putting up the tack, I brushed the horse, and put him back in the barn. From there, walked over to the bunkhouse. I paused at the door, and knocked.

Lloyd opened the door, "You're the only person that's ever knocked on this door," he chuckled.

"It feels weird to just walk in. This is your home," I explained.

"Fair enough. Come on in. What can we help you with?" he asked, letting the door shut behind me.

"For starters I was curious if Jimmy made it back alive," I smiled.

"Jimmy!" Lloyd shouted back toward the bunks.

"Yeah?" he asked, leaning out to look at me from one of the top bunks.

"Did you lose something today?"

He got up quickly, almost falling off the bed. "My horse threw me off!"

"I figured. I found him, for what it's worth. The bear didn't eat him."

"Oh thank god!"

"You're welcome. He's back in his stall."

"Thank you!"

I was about to head out when Ryan and Colby walked out of the bathroom, wrapped in towels from the waist down. I blushed bright red and looked away.

"Oh come on! I know you're not shy, Charlie!" Colby yelled.

"Is everything okay?" Ryan asked.

"Yeah. I had to come tell Jimmy his horse is just fine," I replied, looking intently at my shoes until I was sure it was safe.

"Everyone is dressed," Lloyd chuckled.

I looked back as Ryan was putting his shoes on. "Did you see the bear?" Ryan asked.

"Not today."

Walker came into the bunkhouse behind me. "Ma'am," he nodded, and went back to his bunk.

"I'm assuming you three found it, if Jimmy got bucked?" I asked.

Jimmy nodded.

"You should have seen what happened! He got thrown and crawled up the smallest tree in the forest," Ryan laughed.

"You weren't laughing when it happened," Walker piped up.

"It's funny because no one got hurt," Ryan countered, coming to stand next to me.

"I'm glad no one got hurt," I smiled as he wrapped his arm around my waist.

"Do you want to stay for dinner?" Colby asked.

"Sure." I turned to Ryan and asked quietly, "Is that okay?"

"Of course." He smiled and kissed my cheek. "It's actually my night to cook."

"How can I help?"

"You are a guest! You sit down and have a beer! Make him do all of the work!" Colby said, pulling me away from Ryan, and toward the table.

I laughed as Lloyd grabbed a round of beers from the fridge and passed them out. I sat down next to Lloyd and across from Colby and we started talking about our days.

"Did you find out how Monica was doing?" Ryan asked, turning from the counter.

"She was awake when I took Tate up there, but I didn't actually see her. If I had to guess, she's got a long road to recovery," I explained.

"Sorry to hear that," Lloyd responded.

There was a silent pause before something really started to stink. "What did you manage to burn already?" Colby asked, turning to look at Ryan.

"That is not my fault! There's shit down in the grates because you didn't clean up last night," Ryan shot back.

I looked at Lloyd, "It truly is a miracle that you've managed to keep them alive this long."

"You have no idea, darlin'."

...

Just as we were sitting down to dinner, the door opened, and Beth and Tate stepped inside. "I wondered where you were," she said.

"Hey Tate, I didn't think you'd be back quite yet," I smiled.

"Can we join you for dinner? I don't cook, and he's hungry," Beth explained.

"Yeah, come on in," Lloyd said, beckoning them over to the table.

"I made beef stew," Ryan told her.

"Will you eat that?" Beth asked Tate, who nodded.

Tate and Beth sat down as Ryan called everyone else over to get dinner.

"Let's hope it's edible," Colby teased.

Ryan turned and glared at him in response.

"I'll be the brave one to try it first. If I keel over, don't eat it," I laughed. I got up and Ryan handed me a bowl. "I have total faith, Baby," I whispered, kissing his cheek quickly. "It looks good."

"It actually does look good," Jake commented from over my shoulder, as I put the bowl down on the table.

With a little bit of mock fear I took a bite of the stew, and it was pretty good. It was comparable to something I'd make myself.

"Well?" Beth asked.

"It's good," I smiled.

"Oh hell yes!" They all rushed the stove to get dinner.

"Hold it!" Lloyd hollered. "Guests first."

Ryan dished up bowls for Beth and Tate, passing them over to where they sat at the table. "Chef's next," he announced. "Then you can fight over it." Once he got his food, he came back to the table. "Can I sit by you?"

"I was kinda hoping you would," I smiled.

He sat down and I put my hand on his knee under the table.

"So you're the one my sister is seeing?" Beth asked as everyone started to sit down to dinner.

He paused, looking sideways at me.

"We are the worst kept secret on this ranch." Honestly, knowing that my dad knew, and didn't care, made everything so much easier. "Beth, this is Ryan. Ryan, this is my tornado of a sister."

"Nice to meet you, ma'am."

"Don't ever call me ma'am again, and we'll get along just fine," she smiled.

He nodded and dinner went along, with all of the cowboys giving each other a hard time. After dinner, I helped Ryan with the dishes while Walker got out his guitar to play for Beth.

When we were done Ryan sat down at the table, and pulled me onto his lap, wrapping his arms around me. "Did I pass the test?"

"My test is the only test you have to pass, and you passed that a while ago," I smiled.

I felt him smile as he kissed my neck. It was a good night, shooting the shit and listening to Walker sing. We were still there when Rip came into the Bunkhouse later that evening.

"I need your help, Charlie." The look on his face said something was very wrong.

# Chapter 16

I got up from Ryan's lap and followed Rip out the door. "What's wrong?" I asked.

"I can't find your dad. I've called and left him messages, and he's not responding." Rip goes on to tell me that while he was out looking for the bear, he found a couple of tourists hanging off a cliff on our land. In the process of attempting to save the tourists, one slipped and fell to their death, and after that, the other one jumped. Then to make a bad situation worse, the bear appeared and charged Rip.

"I had to shoot it. It was self-defense."

"I believe you," I replied. "Have you checked the house yet?"

"No, I haven't been up there yet. We need to call the Sheriff, and Fish and Wildlife. I won't do that before he knows about it," Rip explained.

"Let's start with the house, and then we'll go from there." When we got to the house, I jogged up the front stairs and opened the door. Rip was behind me, but hesitated at the threshold. I turned, "Rip, you don't need anyone's permission to be in here. You're family."

"I'm afraid you're the only one that feels that way, Charlie, but I appreciate that you think of me that way," he said, coming in and closing the door.

"I don't think I'm the only one," I replied. I turned and called out for my father.

"What are you screaming for, Charlotte?" My father appeared at the railing on the floor above us.

"We have two dead tourists and a dead bear. Rip said we needed to tell you before we call the relevant authorities," I explained.

"Hang on." He came downstairs, but he was moving slower than normal.

"Are you okay?" I asked.

"I'm fine." He looked at Rip, "I want you to walk me through what happened before we call." My father gestured for us to follow him into his office. At least I thought I was included. "You can go, Charlotte." He stopped me at the door after Rip was inside.

"Why?" I asked.

"I don't want you mixed up in this," he replied, and closed the door in my face.

I huffed and decided to go home. When I made it back, the dogs were waiting for me on the porch. I let them inside, and texted Ryan to let him know I wasn't coming back tonight.

***The Sheriff didn't come out until the next morning. I directed him to the house, when he came down to the barn looking for my father and/or Rip.

Ryan found me while I was in the barn, feeding my horse. "Am I allowed to ask if everything is okay?" he asked. "You ran out of there pretty quickly last night and now the Sheriff is here."

I looked around to make sure we were alone. Once I was satisfied, I stepped closer. "Keep this to yourself... There were two tourists who got lost. Rip tried to help them, but one slipped, and the other just jumped. That's what the Sheriff is here for. I imagine Fish and Wildlife will be here today too, because Rip shot the bear when it charged him last night."

"Holy shit," Ryan mumbled.

"And when I tried to help, I was turned away because my father didn't want me mixed up in it." I rolled my eyes.

Ryan pulled me into a hug and I felt myself relax. "Maybe it's for the best?" he suggested. "I actually have something you can help with."

I pulled back and raised an eyebrow at him. "We are not having sex in the barn in broad daylight," I replied.

"That's not what I need help with!" he laughed, letting me go. "The Bunkhouse wants to chip in and get Jimmy a new hat. We were hoping you could order it and go pick it up."

I smiled, "That's really sweet. I'd love to help. Do you guys have something specific in mind?"

"Almost anything is better than that scarecrow straw hat he wears," he replied. He handed me a paper with Jimmy's hat size scribbled down on it.

"What about something classic, and simple? Just a plain black hat?" I asked.

"That's perfect!"

"Just let me know when you're ready for me to put the order in, and I'll get it done," I smiled. I liked the idea of having a task I could complete.

"Do you have time to go today?" Ryan asked.

"Yeah. It'll be nice to get out of here for a bit." I pulled him in for a quick kiss, and headed for my car. I pulled out my phone and called the shop in town to make sure they had what I needed before I left. The clerk took several minutes to go look, before coming back to tell me they had a black hat in Jimmy's size in stock. I asked them to hold it for me, because I would be heading into town today.

I drove into town, blasting the music on the radio, and trying not to think about how mad I truly was at my dad.

My first stop was the shop to pick up Jimmy's hat. Once I was done with that, I decided that I wasn't ready to go home. It was almost lunch time, so I decided to stop into Beth's new office.

I parked in front of the building, and hopped out of my car. When I stepped into the office, a young man about my age stood up from his desk and greeted me. "Sorry, do you have an appointment?" he asked. He looked a little bit scared.

"She doesn't need one!" Beth called from her desk. "That's my sister, Charlie."

"I'm so sorry," the man stammered.

"It's okay. I did drop in unannounced," I smiled, and walked back toward Beth's desk.

"To what do I owe the visit in the middle of the day?" Beth asked as I dropped down in the chair in front of her desk.

"I had to come into town to grab something for the wranglers, and I thought I'd come see the new office," I replied.

"You ran out of the bunkhouse pretty quick last night. I think your man was a little bit upset you didn't come back," she teased. "What happened?"

I recounted Rip's story about the two tourists and the bear.

"I'm sensing some irritation," she said as she lit a cigarette.

I chuckled, "Only some?"

"Hang on, before you tell me what has you all riled up, what do you want for lunch? Jason can order it and go get it."

"I don't care," I replied. "You pick."

"Jason," Beth called, getting his attention. Once he was standing just behind me, she told him to order a couple salads from one of the restaurants in town. She also asked him to pick up two iced coffees.

"Got it."

"How many times growing up did we hear Dad say that we needed to step up and learn how to run the ranch?" I asked.

"Too many."

"I didn't realize that it didn't really apply to me." I rolled my eyes. "Apparently, all I'm good for is taking care of the animals. He was never happy with how Lee did it, Jamie's an attorney, and Kayce doesn't live here anymore. God forbid I try to do what he's asked us to do all our lives."

"What brought this on?" Beth asked.

"He turned me away when I tried to help last night."

"You don't want to be the one that runs the ranch, Charlie. You don't want those problems. You could do so much better than being stuck on that ranch until he's forced to sell it - because it's when, not if," she explained.

"Are the finances really that bad?" I asked.

"It's more of an issue about the property that's being developed next door. It could be a big problem. He asked me to stay, and try to prevent that development."

"Wow... I'll take dealing with the animals over your job any day," I replied.

"Don't be too hard on yourself. By virtue of our gender, you and I were never meant to have any kind of leadership position. Make yourself happy. That's all you can do."

"You're not the first person to tell me that."

Jason came back with lunch and we ate at Beth's desk before I left, telling her I'd see her at home.

When I got back to the ranch, I texted Ryan, and asked him where I should meet him to hand off Jimmy's new hat.

Lloyd is in the barn, Colby and I are keeping Jimmy busy.

I'll head over to the barn.

I found Lloyd right where Ryan said he'd be. He and Walker were brushing their horses down before they could go back in their stalls. "Lloyd, Ryan told me I should give this to you." I held up the box.

"Damn, you're quick!"

"Shopping is one of my special skills," I laughed, handing it off. Ryan had mentioned a plan to take the old hat before giving him the new one. He'll totally freak out once he realizes his hat is gone. "You'll have to tell me what his reaction is."

"Come down and play poker with us tonight, and you can see for yourself," Lloyd offered.

"I just might." My phone went off, and I looked down, it was my dad, telling me to come up to the house. "I have to go."

"Thanks for your help. We'll get you the money the next time you come down," Lloyd told me.

"Thanks!"

I made it up to the house and found my dad on the porch. "Have a seat," he said, patting the rocking chair next to the one he was already occupying.

"Why do I feel like I'm in trouble?" I asked, sitting down.

"Should you be?"

"I plead the fifth," I replied. "Why did you call me up here? Did everything go okay today?"

My father sighed heavily. "No, it did not. The Fish and Wildlife agent that came to see the bear, ended up impaled on a fence post."

"Jesus Christ! How did that happen?" I asked, staring over at my father, mouth agape.

"I'll let Rip tell that story. They're sending another one out tomorrow. Have you been able to get ahold of your brother today?" He's flipping through what looks like legal documents, so I'm assuming he means Jamie, but I'm going to make him clarify anyway.

"Which one?"

"The lawyer," he replied.

"No, actually." I take my phone out and confirm that my texts from earlier were still unanswered. "I asked what time he'd be back, and nothing."

"So it's not just me he's ignoring," my father grumbled.

"Is there anything I can do to help?" I already knew the answer.

"No."

I was still up at the house later that night when Rip came back in the chopper. "Is she going to be okay?" My father asked about the Fish and Wildlife agent.

"She'll make it," he replied.

"You have to tell me how this happened," I interjected.

"Horse fly bit her horse, and it bolted. She was thrown off and when she fell, she fell on the fence post," Rip replied dryly.

"Are you okay?" I asked.

He smiled, "I'm fine, Charlie."

While we were still outside, Jamie finally came home. I watched as my father flung down the papers that he'd been looking at, and stormed off the porch toward my brother. "Where the fuck have you been?"

"Campaigning. What's wrong?" Jamie replied. He looked up at me with a puzzled look on his face.

"Don't look at her. You're dealing with me. You need to be here tomorrow when Fish & Wildlife comes," my father snapped in Jamie's face.

"Why is Fish & Wildlife coming tomorrow?" Jamie asked.

"You'd know if you'd bothered to pick up your phone!" My father snapped.

"Christina has my phone. I have campaign stops tomorrow. I can't cancel!"

"You can and you will! You're dropping out of the race!"

"Dad?" I asked, from the porch.

He swung around, "Stay out of this, Charlotte!"

Before I knew what was happening, Jamie had a hand on my dad's arm, pulling him back to face him. They were shouting about the campaign, and then my dad punched Jamie in the face, knocking him to the ground.

"Stop!" I screamed, lunging forward.

Rip was faster than I was, and pulled my father off of my brother. "Until you can put family first, you're not welcome on this ranch!" My father snapped as Rip pulled him off.

Rip stood in between Jamie and my father, facing Jamie.

I opened my mouth to say something, but he cut me off. "You're next if you say one more word."

I held my hands up in surrender and walked away and headed to my cabin. I'll go to Jamie's office tomorrow and we can talk about it then.

As expected, the dogs were waiting on the porch when I got back to my cabin. I let them inside and threw a bag of popcorn in the microwave.

I wasn't going to take my bad mood to the bunkhouse.

# Chapter 17

I changed while my popcorn was still popping, and once it was done, I curled up in bed with the dogs. I turned on the tv, trying to distract myself. I heard my phone vibrate on the nightstand. I rolled over and picked it up.

Ryan: Jimmy likes his new hat, but Dipshit put it on the bed two seconds after getting it.

Charlie: I'm glad he likes it, but that's some bad luck.

Ryan: Is everything okay? I thought you were going to come play poker tonight.

Charlie: I'm grouchy and didn't want to bring my bad mood to the bunkhouse. More family drama bullshit.

Ryan: Want me to come cheer you up?

Charlie: I wouldn't say no, but you don't have to if you don't want to.

Ryan: I want to. I'll be right there.

I reminded Ryan where the spare key was hidden so he could let himself in and I wouldn't have to get out of bed.

About twenty minutes later, I jumped when I heard the key turn in the lock. "Charlie?" I heard him call out as he took off his shoes.

"Back here!" I replied. I made the dogs move to give him room to get in bed with me, and put the popcorn bowl on the nightstand.

"What happened?" Ryan asked, coming back into my room.

" I just watched my dad beat the crap out of Jamie for doing exactly what he was told to do," I mumbled.

He took his sweatpants off and got in bed. We took a moment to resituate, so that he had an arm around me, and my head was on his chest. "Did he really put his hat on the bed?" I asked, yawning.

"Oh yeah. He had it for less than two minutes."

"He's a few crayons short of a full pack," I giggled. "We'll have to work on that."

"If he doesn't accidentally hurt himself first," Ryan chuckled.

"Don't put that out into the universe," I teased. "He's uncoordinated enough that he doesn't need help from the universe to do that."

We laid in silence for a while, and I almost thought Ryan had fallen asleep on me when there was a creak in the other room. "What was that?" he asked, sitting up.

"It's just the cabin settling," I replied.

"That sounded like a footstep," he countered.

"Did you lock the door when you came in?"

"Yes."

"Then there's no one out there."

"How do you know?" Ryan asked.

"Because they'd have to break a window to get inside. And I've lived here long enough to know what sounds are normal for here," I yawned.

"Do you believe in ghosts?" he asked, settling back down, leaning up on one arm.

"Do you?" I replied, looking up at him.

"I've seen things on this ranch I can't explain," he said.

"Like what?"

"I've seen a blond woman in a white dress. From afar, I thought it was you, but she disappeared in front of my eyes when I called out to her."

"Where was she?" I asked.

"Over by the cemetery."

"Long blond hair? Down, not pulled up?" I asked. I've seen a younger woman in white with her hair down, and an older woman with her darker blond hair pulled up.

"Down. You've seen her too?" Ryan replied. "Who is she?"

"I have my theories, but I don't know for sure."

"Who do you think it is?" Ryan finally laid all the way back down.

"I think it's Elsa," I yawned. "Her grave is the oldest one in the cemetery. The story I've been told is that she picked the location of the original homestead."

"Isn't your middle name Elsa?" he asked.

"It is."

"I didn't know it was a family name."

"From what I've been able to find out, she really lived in the short time she was here."

"How do you know?"

"I found old family journals in the attic of the lodge when I was sixteen."

"That's cool." He rubbed slow circles into my back as I fell asleep.

***

He was still there when my alarm went off in the morning. A few seconds later we heard a clap of thunder, and rain pouring down on the roof. "This would be a great day to stay in and do nothing if we didn't work and live on a ranch," I chuckled.

"This should clear up by noon," he replied, leaning over to kiss me before getting out of bed.

"I'm joining you guys for roping practice this afternoon," I told him as I got out of bed. "I'm going to shower, so I'll see you later today." I pulled him in for one last kiss before I headed for the bathroom, and he left for the bunkhouse.

I showered and I got dressed for the day, jeans and a black long-sleeved shirt, with my favorite boots and matching hat. Ryan let the dogs out when he left so they could run to the barn for breakfast.

Around 10am, I ran through the rain up to the main house to go get my car so I could go into town to talk to Jamie. I hoped things had calmed down after last night, and that he'd be coming home soon. That was a crack dream.

I walked into his campaign office, to find him and Christina talking animatedly in a back corner. "What do you want?" she snapped at me when she saw me.

"To have a conversation with my brother," I snapped back.

"If you're here to kick me while I'm down, Beth has already done that this morning," Jamie said. "I can't take much more." He had bruises on his face, a busted lip, and gash on his cheek.

"If you really think so little of me, you can fuck right off." I flung my hands up and stormed out.

I made it back to the ranch in time to saddle my horse and make it to the arena for roping practice. I was paired with Jimmy; he was heading, and I was heeling. We didn't get very far because as he was tying off his rope, his saddle came off his horse, and it and he were being dragged around the arena by the cow.

"Let go!" I yelled in unison with everyone else.

When he finally let go of the saddle, he rolled to a stop and was gasping for air. "It's because I put my hat on the bed!" He yelled.

"It's because you didn't take care of your tack," Rip replied. "It's got nothing to do with luck!"

I got down from my horse and looked down at Jimmy, "Are you okay?" I asked.

"Where's my hat?"

I looked around and found it a few inches away from him. "It's right there," I pointed.

"Thank you."

"Anyone care if I cook for y'all tonight?" I asked, looking around at the rest of the group.

"Please save us from Jake's cooking!" Colby called.

"You said you liked my stew the last time I cooked!" Jake snapped.

"She's a better cook than all of us!" Colby replied.

"You can cook for us if you'll stay and play poker after dinner," Lloyd cut in.

"I can do that," I smiled.

We eventually reset and went several more rounds before we called it an afternoon. I put my horse away and went to the bunkhouse to figure out what I could make, while the guys finished their afternoon chores.

***

After dinner, Lloyd made Jake and Ethan clean up the dishes while the rest of us sat down to play poker. "You're going to learn just how much your boyfriend sucks at this game," Colby chuckled as he started dealing cards.

"He can't be that bad," I giggled.

"No, he is," Lloyd said.

"Really?" Ryan asked.

"What? We always trash talk when we play," Colby grinned.

"Shut up and deal."

We were four hands in when Rip came in with a young woman who was carrying a couple bags with her. "This is Avery," Rip said. "I want you to treat her like a cowboy. Understand?"

"I thought you said there weren't any other girls?" Avery asked.

"I don't actually live in the bunkhouse. I'm Charlie Dutton," I replied.

"Okay." She turned back to the guys, "Can someone point me to an empty bunk?" Once Rip was satisfied, he backed out of the bunkhouse.

"Back right on the bottom," Lloyd replied.

"Bathroom?" Avery asked.

Colby pointed to the door.

She walked back to her bunk and put her stuff down. The guys,including Ryan, all got up and followed her. I stayed seated at the table, content to watch this play out from a distance.

"Didn't you used to be a...," Colby trailed off.

"Yep." Avery took her pants off while they all stood around and watched. "I'm not sure why you're all nervous. I've had my ass in every face in this room, except her's." From the context I finally inferred that she used to be a stripper.

With little warning, she pulled off her shirt too. "I will cut your dick off if I wake up to anyone trying to get in bed with me. Got it?" There was stunned nodding from the group. "Give me fifteen, and deal me in." She grabbed a towel and went to the bathroom.They all looked around at each other, dazed. "I'm gonna guess that no one saw that coming," I said. Ryan shook his head. "Come on, let's keep playing," I said, coaxing them back to the table.

Avery joined us a few hands later, and we kept playing. Colby was right. Ryan was horrible at poker. I was about to tease him about it when the door opened, and in walked Kayce.

"What are you doing here?" We both asked at the same time.

CPSIA information can be obtained
at www.ICGtesting.com
Printed in the USA
LVHW050235040223
738616LV00016B/1855

9 781805 092056